Pools of Blue

Pools
of
Blue

SUE RYAN

Matador
Unit E2 Airfield Business Park,
Harrison Road, Market Harborough,
Leicestershire. LE16 7UL
Tel: 0116 2792299
Email: books@troubador.co.uk
Web: www.troubador.co.uk/matador
Twitter: @matadorbooks

ISBN 978 1 80313 302 7

British Library Cataloguing in Publication Data.
A catalogue record for this book is available from the British Library.

Printed and bound in Great Britain by 4edge Limited
Typeset in 11pt Minion Pro by Troubador Publishing Ltd, Leicester, UK

Matador is an imprint of Troubador Publishing Ltd

For Patrick and Alex; my love always for the wonderful young men you've become, and my total admiration for everything you've achieved to date and will, I have no doubt, go on to achieve in the future.

For Nick; forever in my heart.
Thank you for all the lovely memories.

Chapter One

The nurse handed me my discharge letter. It was sealed and addressed to my GP. The accompanying list of prescription drugs was not sealed, and it made for some unsettling reading. Apparently my Consultant had deemed me recovered enough to be released. Well what did he know? Parts of me had recovered, granted, but I reckoned my heart was still in intensive care, refusing to play ball with this whole 'getting better' thing. Nonetheless it managed to produce an impressive ECG printout, one sufficient enough to fool the whole medical team. One month and four days ago, there seemed little hope of any part of me surviving the wreckage. But time, as they say, is a great healer. And modern medicine is a sodding marvel.

You see one month and four days ago, my husband shot me. Or should I say my soon-to-be-ex-husband shot me. Call me sensitive, but I decided that I no longer wanted to be with him after he'd pumped a couple of bullets into my body. So I filed for divorce. I say bullets but actually they were pellets. Otherwise I wouldn't be here at all. Also I did no such filing, my sister took care of the details and I just signed on the dotted line with, it has to be said, some difficulty due to the plaster cast encasing my whole right arm. I was told that one pellet hit my shoulder and the other my thigh, so it took me a good while to figure out why my arm was smashed to bits. Turns out I'd keeled over from the impact of the pellets (pretty pathetic, I know). Our coffee table had broken my fall, along with my right arm. Ironically, that table had been a wedding present from Chris's Mum and I'd always hated it.

So here I was, fully 'recovered' and ready to face the world again. How exactly does one face the world when one has been shot by one's husband? I guess I was about to find out. But first let me try and explain exactly how I came to be in this unfortunate position.

***

LONDON 1997

Of course the whole sorry tale began the minute I laid eyes on my husband-to-be, just a few months into my first proper job. After a couple of expensive creative writing courses and free work placements, not to mention a degree and a Masters, I'd finally managed to land the job of my dreams; copywriter for a large Advertising Agency in London. I'd blagged my way into a work placement a few months earlier. Actually I'd *flirted* my way in but hey, the end justifies the means in my book. Either way I proved my worth and so was taken on as a full-time and, to the tangible relief of my parents, salaried member of staff. I felt on top of the world! I had a real job! What's more I was being paid for something I loved doing.

Creative teams generally worked in pairs to dream up an idea in answer to a client's brief. I was teamed up with an experienced Art Director so that he could 'hold my hand' for the first few months. Phil was an avuncular sort, with a bulging belly and a receding hairline. When it turned out that he was taking his own brief a little too literally, I was pretty pissed off. Trust me to cop a sleazebag as my very first creative partner. I really was only interested in his artistic talents vis-a-vis creating TV commercials, not how creative he could be in the bedroom. Might have had something to do with his paunch and lack of hair (the man was only mid-thirties for Christ's sake) but of course I refrained from pointing that out. His chat-up line went something like:

"Hey Sarah, why don't we put this baby to bed tonight at my place, over a bottle of wine? We've nearly cracked it and I definitely think better after a good meal and a glass or two of Merlot."

'If that were the case you should be knee-deep in awards by now' was the riposte that immediately came to mind, but I replied: "Yeah, right Phil. Umm, I don't think that's a good idea really. We'd be better off keeping our relationship professional don't you think?"

"OK sweetheart, but if you change your mind I'm all yours. We could make beautiful music together!"

This was one of many dreadful clichés the man endlessly churned out. Good job I was the writer.

Anyway he got the message loud and clear, and much to my surprise subsequently fell in love with Tina in Accounts. That was a result all right. Because truth be told, I really enjoyed working with Phil. He had a great deal of experience and was a good mentor. I learned a lot from him. We went on

3

to develop a sound working relationship as well as becoming great mates. I never missed an opportunity to tease him about his odious seduction attempt though.

Around about the time that Phil fell hook, line and sinker for Tina (I'm sure it was because she was very understanding about his hugely inflated monthly expenses) the Agency appointed a new Creative Director. A lot of gossip preceded his arrival. He'd been poached from a competitor and his reputation was legendary. Legendary for two reasons I might add; one, if he thought the client was wrong he told them so in no uncertain terms, and two, he could apparently bed any woman he wanted. I'd never met the man and so was more than a little intrigued, whilst at the same time sure of my conviction that his charm wouldn't work on me. No Siree!! If he thinks he's going to get me into bed, he's got another think coming.

And so Christopher Hobson bowled into the Agency and into my life. Tall, dark and – yes you've got it – handsome – he was charm personified. For the first few days anyway. He went around introducing himself to everyone, took a look at some of our work, commented favourably and moved on. All the while smiling at everyone he came into contact with (even the client service boys or 'suits' as we called them). We were all taken in. Clearly the gossip was wrong! Either that or he'd had a massive personality change somewhere between leaving his last Agency and joining ours. Unfortunately, it wasn't too long before the real Mr Hobson emerged.

To be fair to the man (not an easy thing to say about a person who's levelled a gun at you) he did treat his creative teams quite well. He was generally very encouraging and supportive. If he didn't like what you'd produced, his observations were short and not so sweet. But if he did like it the flow of compliments would be nigh on embarrassing. Client meetings, though, were a veritable spectator sport at times. Those present were frequently treated to his famed temper. 'Don't make Chris cross' was the oft-whispered phrase, just prior to one of these meetings. Thinking back, it was amazing how we managed to keep hold of some of our clients. He would make mincemeat of them if they didn't like the ideas he was presenting. He would belittle them, tell them they didn't know what they were talking about and then simply walk out. Invariably, a senior 'suit' was sent to sweet-talk him back to the room where a gibbering wreck of a client apologised to him profusely, saying 'of course he was right, they could see what he meant now – they just hadn't thought of it from that angle...'

This didn't happen at every meeting of course, but on the odd occasion when it did, word would spread like wildfire that Chris had one of the clients cowering in a corner again. This amused the rest of us no end and, in the time-honoured fashion of any Ad Agency worth its salt, work was forgotten for the remainder of the day and everyone made their way to the pub. Everyone in the Creative Department that is, the more responsible members of staff were not given to abandoning their posts in the middle of the day.

Chapter Two

The pub was like a second home to me in those days. Somehow we all managed to convince ourselves that we deserved a few drinks on an almost daily basis at any given hour. Advertising was like that; we worked hard and we played hard. When the pressure was on, say if we had a New Business pitch coming up, life as we knew it would be put on hold until everyone was happy with the presentation that would hopefully win the account. Once over, and especially given a successful outcome, everyone naturally adjourned to the pub for a collective pat on the back and several vodkas and tonic. Youth has an amazing capacity for, well booze obviously, but also for rewarding oneself. A rather selfish notion that I suppose gradually recedes with the passing of years and the taking on of more responsibility. Oh to be eternally young and never know the stress of mortgages, children, 'dry periods' and life-changing decisions.

But I digress. Let's return to Mr Christopher Hobson, the man who was rapidly taking up more space in my head than I deemed desirable. It seemed the more I told myself I wasn't interested in this man, with his big, blue eyes and his easy, affable smile, the more time I spent thinking about him. 'Out damned spot, out I say!' Nope, it didn't work. I had to resign myself to the fact that I was clearly quite taken by him. But I didn't want to be. The man had a reputation. I was worried about what people might think if they knew that I fancied him.

During his first few weeks at the Agency, the odd rumour of his renowned womanising had reached my ears. To me though, he seemed more engrossed in his job than in getting his end away. The Agency was very busy. He had a fair bit on his plate juggling sundry major accounts as well as several capricious creatives. Of course he could have had a string of women outside work whom he met on a strictly rotational basis…but I doubt he had the energy.

Our relationship at the start was wholly a business one. I did my best to avoid looking at him during meetings. For his part, he only seemed interested in my work, not in me as a member of the opposite sex. I concluded that he was very professional. Either that or he didn't find me attractive. No, clearly it had to be the 'very professional' option.

Occasionally he raised his voice to me when he felt I wasn't giving 100%, and every so often I surprised him (not to mention myself) by responding in kind. This invariably prompted him to unleash his easy, affable smile and…damn it! His easy, affable smile should have been outlawed. It should have been hung out to dry, put in stocks or laid bare in the village square for a bit of stoning from the locals.

Then, one day, during a particularly mass-congratulatory session in the pub, he was suddenly at my side. Sure, I'd seen him in the pub a few times before but he'd never spoken to me. Shot me a few of those smiles all right, but let's not get started on the smiles again. So there he was, in my face, asking me what I was drinking. 'Alcohol. And lots of it!' was my school-girlish reply. He just smiled; yep, you've got it, one of his…you know the rest. 'Um, Vodka and Tonic please.' I stuttered. He got our drinks and then I found myself being steered over to a quiet corner of the cavernous pub. To be honest, I hadn't even noticed that they had tables and chairs and a 'round the corner' bit. I'd only ever propped the bar up or propped someone else up next to it. We sat down together and immediately started talking. I can still remember our first proper conversation.

"So, sweet Sarah, you're quite the little enigma. What is it that turns you on?"

"Turns me on?" I giggled, in a rather high-pitched voice. "You mean other than writing scripts for Domestos and Tampax?"

"Yes. I mean what do you like doing? What gives you a thrill?"

As chat-up lines go, I have to admit it was rather different, if slightly unnerving.

"I love the outdoor life. I cycle, I run, I walk in the park. If the weather's halfway decent, I have to be outside. Probably got something to do with the fact that I live in a claustrophobic first floor flat where there's barely room to swing a mouse, never mind a cat."

"I think the tail would come off."

"What?"

"If you swung a mouse – I have a vision of its tail coming off."

"Cats have tails too."

"Yeah, but they're rather more robust than a mouse's tail don't you think?"

At this point I laughed. I didn't really know what else to do. I'd noticed the corners of his mouth twitching whilst we spoke, so I knew it was a game. He laughed too and we shared a look. You know, one of those looks.

"Seriously though, where do you live?"

"Battersea. South of the river, natch."

"Me too, – I'm Richmond. And do you live alone?"

"Nope. I share what little space I have with a rather neurotic flatmate who practises limbo dancing as a hobby."

Now it was his turn to laugh. "Why, pray?"

"No idea. Maybe it's to help her contort her body so that she can fit into the cupboard under the stairs – or the second bedroom as the Landlord prefers to call it."

He chuckled again and yes, we shared another of those looks.

And so the afternoon turned into evening. We hardly noticed the hours slipping by. Neither did it occur to either of us to return to the Agency. Nobody bothered us; I guess all our colleagues went their separate ways at some point during the evening. I didn't really clock it at the time, but when I think back on this, our first social encounter, I remember Chris worked his way through two bottles of red wine to my four vodkas and tonic. I didn't clock it because it didn't seem to have much effect on him. It was clearly something that his body was used to.

The easy chat went on, accompanied by some silly laughter and some outrageous flirting (on my behalf – I'm pretty good when I want to be). He started paying me compliments at some point during the evening. OK maybe the wine had affected him after all. He said I was extremely attractive and very sexy in an unassuming way. I just giggled at that of course. But when he complimented me on my writing talents, I blushed. That really meant a great deal to me.

By the end of the evening, I was convinced I was in love with him. Outside the pub, he nabbed a taxi and we both fell into it laughing and holding on to each other. The driver gave us a wary look in his rear-view mirror but must have decided that we weren't the vomiting-in-the-back-of-a-cab type as he greeted us with a 'Where to lovers?' Before I could speak, Chris had given him his address in Richmond. I opened my mouth to say something but was immediately silenced by a kiss. Not from the cab driver you understand; from Chris. A soft, gentle, full-lipped kiss – not what I was expecting at all. I responded and then we drew apart and I giggled nervously. He took my face in his hands, looked at me with his beautiful pools of blue and kissed me again. Harder this time but still beautifully sensual. In that ridiculous storybook fashion, I really felt that time was suspended. At some point, mid-suspension, we arrived at his flat. He went to pay the driver but I interjected:

"No Chris. I'm not coming in. Not tonight. We've had a great evening – I'll see you tomorrow."

He looked stunned for a second but to his credit just kissed me again and said "I look forward to it." With that he was gone and I was on my way to Battersea with a thousand thoughts running through my head. 'Did that really just happen?' 'Did I actually say no?' 'My God girl, you're learning some restraint in your old age.' That sort of thing. Then I ran through the whole evening – remembering things we'd said, stuff we'd laughed at and, most of all, his beautiful blue eyes and that wonderful smile. And his kiss. You see, despite my misgivings at falling for someone like Chris, I knew. I knew he was the one. No doubt about it. But I wanted to be sure that I was the one for him and not just another notch on his bedpost. So I was going to have to play this very cleverly.

It's amazing just how many thoughts you can fit into your head during a cab ride from Richmond to Battersea.

CHAPTER THREE

I swear I awoke the next morning with a smile on my face. As I edged past my wardrobe and eased myself out of the bedroom door, I decided that even the sight of my unbelievably annoying flatmate was not going to get me down today.

"Morning Sarah!" she sang, as she walked on all fours towards the bathroom, pelvis thrust northwards. "Luuuvely day isn't it?"

OK, so I was wrong. The sight of the stupid bitch did get me down. But I was determined that she was not going to completely spoil my morning. Grabbing some breakfast, I hid in my bedroom until she'd limboed out of the bathroom. I showered and dressed and was out of the flat before you could say 'certifiable lunatic'.

On the way to work, my good mood died a little more. This was not an uncommon occurrence. Spending forty minutes 'up close and personal' with strangers never made me feel good. I hated travelling on the underground at rush-hour – it was inhuman and undignified and I was convinced it made everyone turn up to work pissed off. But, I had other reasons this morning for my changing mood. What if it had all been a bit of fun on his part? What if he never mentioned the evening, or the possibility of seeing me again? Well, at least I hadn't slept with the man, oh no, I hadn't given him that satisfaction. Surely I was holding all the cards? Wasn't I?

Finally I was spewed out of the underground station, along with several hundred other sad fuckers, and I began my ten minute walk to the office. Slowly. So slowly in fact that I was going to be late. Late? What did I mean? There was no such thing as a 'creative' being late – we turned up when we wanted to. After all, everyone knew that you should let sleeping creatives lie. It was dangerous to wake them, or to expect them to be able to function normally before around 11:00 a.m. Anyway, however late I was, I'd certainly beat Chris in.

"Well good morning Ms Williams. Overslept did we? Must have been a late night."

Bollocks.

"Morning Chris," I said, in my best casual voice. Which, on reflection, sounded distinctly un-casual.

"Sarah I'd like to talk to you about the next Fairy Liquid ad – could you come and see me please."

"Yep. Sure. Just give me a minute would you?"

I legged it to my office. Shit. Crap. Bollocks. I didn't even work on Fairy fucking Liquid! What did he mean? What was he going to say to me and how the fuck do I deal with it?

I dumped my bag, grabbed a notepad and pen and walked sedately to his office. Sedately as one can whilst hyperventilating.

Of course I found Mr Cool relaxing nonchalantly on his couch, one leg thrown casually over the side and his left arm propping his head up. He appeared to be studying some notes.

13

"Close the door Sarah."

Oh God. What was coming?

"Have a seat."

I perched on the edge of the couch, as far away from him as possible. Mouth dry, heart racing, eyes avoiding his pools of blue.

"Um, I don't quite know how to say this. I'm not usually stuck for words. You've got me all of a fluster Ms Williams." He looked up. "Would you mind sitting on the couch properly? You look like you're about to fall off. It's very distracting. Um, what was I saying?"

Well he wasn't was he? Saying, I mean. Christ this was worse than I thought. He regrets everything that happened (or didn't happen maybe) and, worse still, I think he wants to fire me! I'll get in there first.

"It's OK Chris, I understand. It was a mistake. Let's put it behind us, forget about it – in fact I've already forgotten about it! What have I forgotten about? Don't know, cos I've forgotten! Ha ha!!"

Christ.

"What? No I didn't mean that. What on earth are you saying Sarah?"

Who knows but I was committed now.

"But Chris please don't fire me. I love my job. I'm good at it – you did mean that bit didn't you? You can pretend I don't exist! Well, until you have to speak to me of course. Silly me, that won't work will it. But we can manage – just please don't fire me."

"What are you talking about Sarah? I have no intention of firing you. And as for last night, well that's what I'm trying to say to you. It was special, exciting. I've chatted up plenty of women in my time and kissed even more (that ratio clearly didn't make sense) but you're different. In fact you're amazing. I haven't been able to get you out of my head. So… that's it basically."

That's it basically, the man said. Well it's a good job I'd taken his advice and had moved onto the couch properly. I'd surely be on my backside on the floor by now otherwise. But, despite the firm settee beneath my bottom, I felt very unstable. Both physically and emotionally. I think it's safe to say that I wasn't expecting that.

"For fuck's sake Sarah, say something."

"Um. Yes. Right. Well…"

"You're a wordsmith Sarah, I'm sure you can do better than that."

"I…feel the same! It *was* special. *You're* special. I can't believe it. Wow! Uh…what do we do now?"

At that precise moment, his secretary gave the briefest of knocks and barged into the office.

"Crisis. Mark needs to speak to you now, he says."

Talk about breaking the atmosphere.

"OK – I'll be with him in a minute," Chris said.

"He said now."

"And I said I'll be with him in a minute!" Chris roared.

Exit one pink-faced secretary, surely having just received her first verbal warning.

"So can we meet tonight Sarah?"

"Er, yeah. 'course. Great! Where?"

"Give me your address and I'll pick you up at eight. OK?"

"OK."

CHAPTER FOUR

You can imagine how it went from there. Expensive restaurants, sessions in the pub, gropes in the lift at work, nights spent at each other's flat – that sort of thing. I say nights spent at each other's flat, but it was mainly me spending the night at his. It was an apartment really, not a flat at all. And it was bloody amazing! Massive open-plan lounge/dining room/kitchen with a shedload of light flooding it. As for the master bedroom, well I think it would probably have put Joan Collins' bedroom in the shade. Not that I've ever seen Joan Collins' bedroom, but one can imagine.

On the odd occasion when he stayed at my place, it was inevitable that we would encounter 'the crab'. The poor girl seemed to have no social life whatsoever. Just spent her evenings practising for some imaginary limbo dancing contest. We should have felt sorry for her but she caused us no end of mirth and we frequently had to come up with excuses for our incessant cackling. She must have thought we spent our lives either watching endless comedy programmes or finding each other hysterically amusing. All in all though, there was no contest. Chris's place beat mine hands down.

And so our relationship progressed. It was hilarious when we were eventually found out at work. The gossip machine went into overdrive. Various comments were thrown my way such as, 'Hot date tonight Sarah? Don't worry, I'm sure you won't be in trouble if you get in late tomorrow!!' Oh ha ha.

Then there was the less subtle 'Just had a meeting with your boyfriend Sarah, must have been a good night – he was in a great mood!" Again, ha bloody ha. Phil, though, took the prize:

"Sarah baby, you screwing the boss?"

To which I replied: "Yeah. You got a problem with that?"

"Not if it gets us the best accounts to work on baby, no!"

Good old Phil. Had his priorities right.

As for me, well I was happy as Larry. Truly in love for the first time, over-the-moon, fulfilled. Any doubts I'd had about whether Chris could stay faithful or not were dispelled by the way he doted on me. For heaven's sake, the man was besotted! Understandably of course.

After we'd been going out for about six months, I somehow managed to tear myself away from 'the crab' and move in permanently with Chris. When I told her that she needed to get a new flatmate, I also suggested that she perhaps got a life while she was at it. She looked at me from her usual position of all fours, crotch in the air, and asked in all seriousness, what did I mean? I honestly couldn't be arsed, so just left it hanging there. Much like her crotch.

I feel I should give my parents a mention at this point. They had, of course, met Chris. They'd been to London a couple of times and met us for lunch, and I'd even taken Chris home for a weekend. Something I don't normally do with boyfriends, so Mum knew he was special to me. I'm not sure how special he was to Mum though.

"He seems quite nice dear, but he does drink a lot doesn't he?"

"Mum, I drink a lot." I immediately regretted my confession. "Well, quite a lot that is. We're in advertising, it's what we do."

"Yes dear, I know, but can he control his drinking? Does he drink every day?"

Is the Pope Catholic?

"He's fine Mum, don't worry."

"Well I'm happy for you, of course, but just be careful."

Parents. What do they know?

A fair bit, as it turned out.

So, back to my loved-up self and my wonderful Chris. It does seem a shame to spoil the romantic reverie doesn't it, but I'm afraid that's exactly what I'm about to do.

Against all odds, we managed to live together and work together without any major fallouts for, ooh…at least three months. The first crack appeared one night when I decided to go home from the pub at closing time (not an unreasonable course of action) but Chris wanted to stay on and drink with some of his buddies. So I got a taxi and left him there. Big mistake. I was awoken at around 4:30 a.m. to the sound of him banging his fists on the apartment door. So loudly that he woke not only me but several of our, to that point, very accommodating neighbours. God only knew what he'd done with his key. I quickly pulled him inside with an apologetic smile at said neighbours who were peering around their doors, and muttered some words to the effect of 'tough day at work…we lost some business…so sorry.'

Once in the apartment he headed straight for the drinks cabinet. Obviously. Because that was clearly what he needed – a drink.

"Chris you aren't seriously having another one are you? For Christ's sake, you can barely stand up!"

"Yes I am having another one, what the hell does it look like you stupid fucking bitch?"

I looked around the room to see who he was talking to, 'cos clearly it couldn't have been me. He wouldn't speak to me like that. He'd NEVER spoken to me like that. Except there was no one else in the room and it *was* me he was talking to. For a second or two, my body didn't seem to be receiving any messages from my brain. Eventually, my legs started moving and I walked to our bedroom as steadily as I could. Once inside, I locked the door to make it quite clear to him that he would not be sharing my bed for what little remained of that night.

Chapter Five

It's funny how life can continue relatively normally when you've got a little voice inside your head blethering at you constantly. The next day was interesting, to put it mildly.

I awoke later than usual and had that brief second of nothingness until all the events of the previous night came flooding back. I showered and dressed and made my way towards the living area with some trepidation. The closer I got to the kitchen, the more I became aware of both a wonderful aroma and a strange, rather jolly noise. It turned out to be Chris whistling. Yep – my drunken, belligerent, foul-mouthed boyfriend was making fresh coffee and attempting a version of 'When You're In Love With A Beautiful Woman'. How was he not comatose on the settee? Or suffering from a raging hangover? The man was not human.

"Morning darling – coffee?"

Oh yes Chris. I'll see your coffee and I'll raise you 'STUPID FUCKING BITCH!'

I took my cup without saying a word and turned away. I was NOT going to make the first move in this fucked-up scenario.

"Sarah, about last night. I'm truly sorry."

"Which bit are you truly sorry for Chris? Getting legless?

Waking all the neighbours? Having another drink when you could barely stand? Or calling me a 'stupid fucking bitch'?"

He had the grace to wince at that last bit.

"Christ, all of it Sarah. I was out of order. I was wrong."

I waited. There had to be more. This was not cutting it with me.

"I was having such a good time with the boys last night. I didn't realise how much I was drinking or how late it was. We had such a laugh, honestly!"

Oh that's OK then Chris – so long as you were having a good time. I guess my look of disgust said it all.

He sighed. "I know I behaved badly. I am so sorry Sarah. Really."

Still I waited.

Nothing.

"You called me a STUPID FUCKING BITCH!!" I yelled.

"Oh God I know, how could I do that? Sarah, sweetheart, please forgive me. I am truly sorry. I love you so much baby."

And then he said those fateful words.

"It won't happen again, I promise."

Well, dear reader, I did forgive him. In time. Oh of course I made him suffer for a while. He had to pay his dues. We talked about it at length. I had to make him see how much he'd upset me and that his behaviour was unacceptable. Whilst he didn't physically fall to his knees in supplication, I could tell that he was hugely sorry for hurting me.

Why do women forgive men who verbally or physically abuse them? Because they love them of course. Because women think that somehow they might be to blame. Because each time it happens, they truly believe that it won't happen again.

Guess what? It happened again.

Chapter Six

Fast forward four or five months. We'd been getting on famously and had put that awful night firmly behind us. Chris still drank of course (as did I) and, if I could have been honest with myself at the time, he drank too much. But he was generally great company under the influence. Sure, he had his low moods and his problems at work which drove him to even more drink, but things never got out of hand. We mainly went to the pub together, with work colleagues or friends, or we shared a bottle of wine at home. Well, I suppose we shared a *couple* of bottles of wine most evenings, although the sharing wasn't exactly equal. If he did stay out late drinking, he spent the night at a mate's place rather than coming home.

Oh I knew what was going on. I knew it was to avoid a repeat of 'that night' at all costs and I was sure he was drinking himself stupid on those occasions, but at least I didn't have to be confronted with it.

So, as I say, a few months on and things were looking good. Chris had booked us a holiday in Venice. I was over the moon – I'd always wanted to go there and it didn't disappoint in the slightest. We spent a week in a fabulous 5 star hotel and did all the usual tourist things, including a ride in a Gondola. Mid said ride, Chris took me (and our less-than-amused Gondolier) completely by surprise by leaping to his feet in the boat (don't try it, just don't). He then went down on one knee and proposed. To me, not the Gondolier. Well of course I said yes! Champagne was produced from somewhere, along with a beautiful engagement ring which fitted me perfectly, and our Gondolier – possibly sensing the prospect of a large tip coming his way – softened and launched into a rendition of 'O Sole Mio'. Or 'Just One Cornetto' to give it its proper title.

Back in grey old England, I tried not to behave like the proverbial cat that had got the cream. But…well, I felt like the proverbial cat that had got the cream. The ring was flashed at every available opportunity at work and was much admired. I have to say though, there were one or two snide comments from a couple of jealous bitches, who apparently saw themselves cheated out of the role of becoming Mrs Christopher Hobson. On what basis pray? My gut instinct was to sneer at them and simply gloat, but I managed a vaguely sincere look of pity as I dispatched the words "don't worry. I'm sure you'll find a husband of your own. One day…"

My parents took the news fairly well. Better than I expected in fact. I guess they could see how happy I was and so they were happy for me. If my mother still harboured any doubts about Chris at the time, she didn't share them. I did wonder what sort of private conversations might be taking place between her and Dad but I was grateful that they kept any negative thoughts to themselves. With hindsight, would I have wanted them to voice their concerns and try and talk me out of it? Nah. Wouldn't have worked would it? I was in love.

Chris took me to his Mum's to tell her the news. I'd met his Mum a couple of times; we'd bonded immediately. She was a sweet, kind lady whose whole word clearly revolved around her only son. Chris's parents had been separated for a number of years and he rarely mentioned his Dad. Whenever I tried to bring up the subject, he'd simply say that he had no wish to discuss him. So that was that. Men…don't you just love 'em? Why can't they open up a bit sometimes like us girls? Well maybe not quite like us girls as that would just be weird – but would it hurt them to talk a little about their feelings? On my first visit to his Mum's house, I did a surreptitious scan of the living room for any possible photos of 'The Ex'. Couldn't see one. Just a plethora of pictures of Chris at various ages and a couple of his sister, Jane. She was living in America at the time, so I didn't get to meet her until the wedding. I didn't feel I could ask his Mum about her ex-husband so I remained in the dark as to what had gone on there.

My friends were ridiculously happy for me. They behaved like a bunch of school girls, screaming and giggling and hugging me. Almost as if I'd been perilously close to forever being on the shelf but had been rescued at the last moment. I was only 27 for God's sake! I think they were just happy because they knew how much I loved Chris. They'd of course socialised with us on many occasions and kept saying we were the 'perfect, beautiful couple'.

You may be wondering at this stage how Chris's drinking was never a concern to my friends. Quite simple really – we all drank a lot. Nobody noticed that he was putting away more than anyone else. Like I said, most of the time it seemed to have little to no effect on him. I guess, looking back, he was in a permanent state of semi-inebriation. You'd think I'd spot that, wouldn't you. Well, you see what you want to see. And I guess you don't see what you don't want to see.

I'd only confided in one friend about 'The Incident'. Becky, my best mate since our college days. We all have that one friend (girls do at least) with whom we do mad things – get drunk, get thrown out of nightclubs, chat up inappropriate men just for the hell of it and flirt outrageously on a 'Girls' Night Out'. Becky, four inches shorter than me, blonde and bouncy, was that friend. We'd shared so many good times together – and the odd, awful 'did I really do that?' time. We were truly kindred spirits. So naturally I had told Becky about what happened.

We were in our favourite wine bar, for a post-work drink one day. After the usual catching up on each other's news, the inevitable giggling and the surreptitious surveying of good-looking blokes, I topped up our wine glasses and said 'Becks, I've got to tell you something.'

"Oh Christ. You're pregnant."

"Err, no. 'Course I'm not. Would I be knocking back this vino like it's going out of fashion if I were?"

"Yes."

"OK, fair point. The thing is – it's Chris. The other night he…"

"He's not having a bloody affair is he?"

"No. Why would you jump to that conclusion?"

"Just going on what you've told me about him – that's all. Sorry. Carry on."

"Well, no, it's worse than that. Or is it? I don't know.

25

Becks, he got so drunk that he called me a stupid fucking bitch!"

Becky almost choked on her wine. "He what?! Sarah – that's not good. How dare he? I'll fucking kill him. What happened?"

"We'd been out – I came home before him and left him drinking with the lads from work. He arrived home at God knows what time in the morning, woke the neighbours by crashing about and then – can you believe this? – started to pour himself a drink! I had the temerity to suggest that this wasn't a good idea and that's when he called me a stupid fucking bitch."

"Did he hit you?"

"Christ no. He'd never do that."

"A couple of weeks ago you might have said he'd never call you a stupid fucking bitch."

"OK – true. But I know he'd never hit me."

"So what did you do?"

"I went to bed and locked the bedroom door."

Becky took another sip of her wine. "What about the next morning?"

"As if it never happened Becks. Unreal. I went downstairs and he was making coffee and *whistling*."

"Fuck. What did you say?"

"Not much – I wanted to see what *he* was going to say. He did apologise – profusely – but it took him a while to see how upset I was. That's shit isn't it? He should have realised that shouldn't he?"

"Yup. Course he should. What a bastard. What you going to do about it Sez?"

"Don't know. What d'you think I should do?"

Becks and I always asked each other's advice when we had 'situations' going on. Didn't always take it of course, but you've got to at least listen to what your mate thinks haven't you?

"Um," she took a slow drink of her wine, now dangerously close to the bottom of the glass. "God I don't know. I need more drink, that I do know."

She filled us up whilst I waited patiently for her pearls of wisdom.

"OK. There's no point me telling you to leave him is there? Cos you love him. So…you'll just have to make sure he knows how much he hurt you and that it can never happen again. Right?"

"Right. I do love him – God Becks, I love him so much, the bastard! How could he speak to me like that?"

"'Cos he was pissed out of his head Sarah. He didn't mean it. Just don't get into a situation like that again with him OK?"

"Yeah, I know. Can we change the subject now? I'm sick of talking about it."

And I was. So we did.

CHAPTER SEVEN

Who the hell invented weddings? A man, clearly. A man who was going to make damn sure he had nothing to do with the organising of any such event. Good God they're a pain in the arse. Chris was in favour of getting married abroad – somewhere like Italy – with just a few friends and close family. I wished afterwards that I'd seen the absolute sense in that, but at the time I felt it would be letting too many people down. If only someone had grabbed me by the shoulders and shouted in my face 'It's *your* wedding. Do it the way *you* want.' Actually Chris did do that, more or less, but I felt an obligation to my parents, who wanted a nice traditional affair for me (with the exception of the wedding dress that is – 'White dress Mum?' 'No, I think cream would be more appropriate darling. White is so virginal isn't it?') and to my extended family who naturally all wanted to celebrate with us.

So off I went, organising our bloody wedding. We decided on a June date for the following year and booked my parents' village church for the service. That was the easy bit. Agreeing on a reception venue was not so painless. I felt that Mum and Dad should have something of a say in it, seeing as they were paying for the damn thing. My father was very traditional you see – even though Chris could afford to pay for our wedding himself, Dad wasn't having any of it. He wanted us to save our money for a nice, big family house. One step at a time Dad.

My parents couldn't see anything wrong with the hotel in the next village as a venue for the reception. If it was good enough for my older sister, it was certainly good enough for me. Given that Caroline had divorced her worthless husband less than two years after their nuptials, I wasn't at all sure that it was the ideal place for ours. Bad omen? Too many memories for Caroline? Just didn't seem right to me. Chris was dead against it anyway; apparently it was too parochial. Whatever that meant. So we carried on our search, viewing about five other potential venues and dealing with sycophantic wedding coordinators until we finally agreed on a hotel about thirty minutes from the church. I say we; Chris and I agreed on it. Mum and Dad thought it was too far for the guests to travel. This was met with incredulity from Chris who'd think nothing of driving half an hour for a good steak. I told him to leave it to me, I would sort it. Safest option by far. I also had to explain to my parents that this hotel was a tad more expensive than Caroline's but that Chris insisted on paying the difference. Say what you like about my Chris (and, believe me, people have had plenty to say about him), he was no skinflint. I managed to make them understand that a thirty minute drive from church to hotel was quite acceptable, but Dad's pride would not let him agree to Chris's offer of money. And so it came to pass that the non-parochial, slightly overpriced and too-far-from-the-church venue was booked for Saturday 16th June.

Life continued fairly blissfully for a while. I took care of all the other wedding arrangements and the months flew by with Chris and I both engrossed in our work. I know you're waiting for me to tell you about the moment when it happened again. In fact I reckon you can guess when that particular bomb detonated but I'm going to leave you in suspense for a while yet.

Amazingly enough, I managed to scoop myself an industry award for one of my TV commercials. It was for Domestos alas, but who cares about the product? It was an award! Chris and I attended the ceremony with a few others from the Agency and nobody was more surprised than I was when Phil's and my ad was read out as the winner. Well, maybe Chris was more surprised. At least, he certainly looked surprised. Or was it annoyed? I couldn't tell, but he quickly hid whatever his first emotion was and gave me a big congratulatory hug and a kiss. Phil and I bounded up to the stage to collect our award, grinning from ear to ear. I glanced back to see Chris pretty much downing his full glass of wine in one gulp. Aww, he's toasting my success, I managed to make myself think at the time. Of course he was.

This was one of the occasions where I opted to go home ahead of Chris and he stayed with a mate in town. No way should the evening have ended like that though. It was MY night. I had won an AWARD! We should have celebrated together and gone home together. But I saw the warning signs and decided not to risk a repeat of the dreaded 'Incident'. Ridiculous when you think back on it. Why the hell did I let him get away with that kind of behaviour?

Of course Becky had to hear all about it, when we next met.

"So proud of you girl…a fucking award!!"

We clinked glasses, sloshing some precious wine over the table; giggled and proceeded to spill some more.

"God Becks, I can't believe it. I NEVER thought I'd win an award. Well not yet anyway. I've only been a copywriter for just over a year! Christ. How did I pull that off??"

"'Cos you're bloody good of course, you silly cow. Well done! Cheers!"

More clinking and spilling, but we did manage to get a little wine down our throats this time.

"What does it mean Sez? Will you get a raise?"

"Nah, doubt it. Mind you, that would be up to Chris. He could always put in for one for me. But I don't think he'll do that."

"Why the hell not?"

"We talked about it once and he said he wouldn't feel right doing that. He'd rather wait until the MD brings up the subject with him."

"Which he might just do now you've won an award!" Becky observed. "So how was the night? What did you wear?"

"Oh my blue dress – you know? The one you spilled your gin and tonic over that night a while back! Remember??"

"God, don't remind me."

"Anyway, it was a pretty good night – OK meal, good company and all that, and Phil and I just couldn't believe it when our names were read out. But Becks, I swear Chris was not happy. I got a jolt when I saw the look on his face."

"How d'ya mean?"

"I swear he looked shocked…no, more than shocked. He looked angry Becks."

"What the hell? Why would he be angry Sez?"

"That's the question I've been asking myself."

Becky leaned in closer to me. "Could he be jealous? Has he ever won any awards?"

"He's won a couple of radio awards, but nothing for TV. They're the big ones."

"Fuck me, Sarah, he's jealous of you."

Becks, as usual, had nailed it. The idea that Chris might be jealous had been floating around somewhere in the recesses of my mind. I simply didn't want to acknowledge it. But Becks was right.

"Did he get drunk and call you names again?"

"Well no. I didn't give him the opportunity. I went home ahead of him and he stayed the night with Dodgy Dan. So I didn't see what state he was in by the end of the evening. When he got back the next day he was absolutely fine."

"That is so wrong girl. It was your night. You should have gone home together. What an arsehole."

"Well it was my decision to go, Becks."

"Yeah, and he let you."

"I know, I know. Am I a complete fucking idiot Becky? Is this whole getting married thing a mistake?"

She took another quick sip of her wine.

"I wish I had a sodding crystal ball Sarah."

CHAPTER EIGHT

So the wedding came and went and, as weddings go, it wasn't really up there with the best. When the day dawned, I could have guessed at what Becky's crystal ball might have revealed for my future. After ten days or so of dry and really quite pleasant English weather, the lead-grey skies facing me were extremely depressing. I had wondered what it was that had awoken me so early. Not feelings of excitement as I first thought, more likely the cats and dogs raining down on my bedroom roof.

Oh it started off well enough. The ceremony was lovely, the choir sang angelically and Chris said I looked beautiful. Well he would, wouldn't he? All brides look beautiful I believe. On the day, I had no doubt about my love for my new husband. Neither did I doubt his love for me. There was just this annoying gnawing kind of feeling in the pit of my stomach which wouldn't go away. I smiled, I laughed, I cried – all the usual permitted emotions for a bride on her wedding day – but every time I caught Becky's eye, we kind of exchanged a look. Becks, to her credit, fulfilled her role as my chief bridesmaid perfectly. She was nothing less than encouraging, complimentary, organised (have to say

33

that particular talent took me completely by surprise) and supportive. But those looks between us said it all.

So where did it all go horribly wrong? I'd say about half way through the groom's third bottle of wine. Chris rarely danced so I'd been having a mad old time on the dance floor with my mates and my family. I sat down for a breather and he put his arm around me and said it was time for him to take me to bed. I giggled and said I didn't want to leave the party yet as everyone was still there and I was having fun. That didn't go down well. It's not as if we were about to experience the particular delights of each other's body for the first time for Christ's sake! That ship had sailed long ago. I wanted to enjoy my wedding. So back I went onto the dance floor, and back he went to his bottle of wine.

A couple of hours later, at around 2:00 a.m., most of the guests had left, or were slumped in a corner somewhere. Time to retreat to our sumptuous bridal suite.

"Hey babe – shall we go up?" I ventured. "Party's good as over!"

"Oh now you want to go to bed with me do you? Wasn't good enough for you a while back was I?"

"Don't be silly Chris, I was just enjoying dancing with my friends. Come on, let's go."

I tried to take his arm but he yanked it away angrily. He was with a couple of his equally drunk mates and they seemed to find this amusing.

"You can go and enjoy your wedding night on your own MRS Hobson. I'm staying here."

I was totally horrified and humiliated. I looked around for some sort of support in the form of Becky, but she'd disappeared with her boyfriend a while back. I tried again:

"Please Chris, don't do this. Come to bed with me."

"No. Staying here with my mates. Fuck off to bed by yourself."

Chapter Nine

You might wonder how our nascent marriage was able to continue after that. Not what you'd call an auspicious start to married life. Should I have high-tailed it out of the hotel there and then? Should I have banged on Becky's bedroom door and begged her to let me into bed with her and Ed? Should I have put an immediate halt on our much-abused bar tab? Well, clearly, the answer to the latter is a resounding 'yes'. I did none of these things though. I went to our luxurious bridal suite and ate all the chocolate-coated strawberries. I then climbed out of my wedding dress, swept the rose petals off the bed, fell onto it and immediately into a deep sleep. How did I manage that you might ask? Well, I was fucking knackered. It had been an extremely busy and somewhat emotional day. I didn't even hear Chris come into the room which he did at, apparently, around 5:00 a.m.

The next morning was interesting. I awoke with a start and, for about two seconds, all was well with the world. Then I remembered. I lay there, churning the events over and over in my mind. Wondering exactly how I was going to deal with this. Chris stirred in his sleep next to me and I panicked. I was saved by a knock on the door though, as our breakfast arrived – complete with red rose and smiling waiter. I grabbed the complimentary fluffy dressing gown with 'Mrs' emblazoned on the back and decided to just eat my breakfast and see what ensued.

Mid-way through my scrambled eggs on toast, Chris opened his eyes and looked at me. It didn't take long for realisation to dawn on him either – although slightly longer than my two seconds I'd say, on account of his alcohol-dulled brain. He sat up slowly, not taking his eyes off me. I waited. Oh boy this better be good.

"Morning Mrs," he ventured.

I gave him an 'are you fucking serious?' look and he quickly continued with:

"I don't remember everything Sarah, but I know I was out of order. What did I do?"

"Ahh you poor thing," I spat (along with some scrambled egg) "lost your memory?"

"Well, I think I remember telling you to go to bed without me. Is that right darling? I'm so sorry."

"No, no, NO Chris!! That is NOT right. Let me remind you of the facts." I shot up and started pacing the room. "Yesterday was our wedding day. Remember that? Last night was our wedding night. You told me to fuck off to bed and have my wedding night by myself. AND, you said it in front of your mates – who seemed to find it hilarious. It was awful Chris, and so humiliating. What the fuck is wrong with you?"

Tears were rolling down my face by now. I spotted the red rose on the breakfast tray, grabbed it and hurled it at him.

"Some fucking wedding night!"

"What can I say babe? I'm so sorry. I didn't know what I was doing. You were off dancing all night so what else was there to do but drink? Please, please forgive me. I love you Sarah."

I faltered. Was I to blame a bit? Should I have spent more of the evening with him rather than with my friends and family? No, I was enjoying myself! So was he though, in the way he knew best.

I sat down on the edge of our prodigious bed and picked up a rasher of stone cold bacon. The ball was well and truly in my court. Now was the time to call a halt to this farce. To walk away with a smidgeon of pride still intact. To file for divorce! How much would I get I wondered? Chris was worth a fair bit, and as his wife surely I was entitled to some of it. No, no, no don't be silly – you've only been married five minutes! And divorce on what grounds? That your new husband didn't want to go to bed with you on your wedding night? I doubt that would hold up in court. I continued turning things over in my mind and toying with the rasher of bacon whilst Chris remained silent, beseeching me with his beautiful pools of blue.

But I was simply playing for time. I knew exactly what I was going to say. I knew what I was going to say even while Chris was verbally abusing me the night before. I wasn't going to give up this easily. Apart from anything else, how on earth could I explain to my parents that our day old (technically speaking not quite a day yet) marriage was over? 'Thanks so much for the fabulous wedding Mum & Dad, it was perfect. Oh, by the way, Chris and I are divorcing...' No, I plainly could not do that. But I had to choose my words carefully. This was his last chance and he had to understand that.

"Chris", I said. "I'm sorry that I spent so much time dancing with my friends and family and not enough time with you. It was our wedding night and I shouldn't have done that."

He opened his mouth to say something but I held up a finger to stop him.

"But, to be fair, firstly you know how much I like dancing and that I rarely have a chance to do it these days. Secondly, we've been living together for a year now for Christ's sake, so it's not like we had to rush to bed for our first night of lust and thirdly…I can't remember what thirdly was going to be."

A smile played around his lips but he wisely didn't allow it to take hold.

He attempted to speak again but up went my School Ma'am Finger once more.

"Let me finish Chris, because this is important. Whatever wrong I did, I did NOT deserve to be belittled and humiliated and SWORN at. I know it was the drink talking, but it's got to stop. You're like Dr Jekyll and Mr fucking Hyde and I can't take it anymore. If you want this fledgling marriage to continue then you have to promise me one thing."

A fly buzzed annoyingly around the room.

"You can speak now Chris."

"Oh, OK…what's that, darling? Promise what?"

"That you get some help with your drinking problem."

"Oh." His head went down. "But I like drinking."

"As much as you like me?"

He shifted the pillow behind his back.

"Well no – obviously not. I love you babe. It's not a fair comparison."

"Well you better start making that comparison," I said. "Because that's your choice. Me or the drink."

God I was proud of myself! Could not believe I'd actually

said it. A deafening silence ensued though. Even the annoying fly had evaporated somehow.

Finally he said "Of course, Sarah, of course I'll do it. I love you so much. You mean more to me than anything."

"Right answer Chris. We'll sort it out straight after the Honeymoon."

"I can drink on our Honeymoon though, right? Please?"

Good God, what had I reduced him to!

"Of course! We'll be together, we'll have fun. Nothing will go wrong – I'll make sure of that." Although I didn't feel quite as certain as I managed to sound.

"OK darling, it's a deal. Now take that ridiculous fluffy dressing gown off and get your sweet arse over here."

CHAPTER TEN

You're probably looking for some kind of Honeymoon horror story now aren't you? Well sorry to disappoint but I can honestly say that our Honeymoon was sublime. Yeah, I know – plenty of opportunity for fuck-ups but we just had a great time together and enjoyed each other's company. He did drink of course – so did I. We drank together and I was impressed with Chris's willpower when we were frequently offered a drink on the house after a meal out. Maybe it was the look I gave him, or possibly the fact that I started caressing his crotch with my bare foot under the table that made him decline the invitation (yes – each time). I'll never know. I think a clue to the answer might be the fact that we had amazing sex on those particular nights. 'Nuff said. Never underestimate the seductive powers of a wily woman.

With the Honeymoon done and dusted, it was back to normality with a (rather limp) bang. Oh it was great to see all my friends again and to share stories of the wedding (especially the one about Chris's Aunt who'd got 'stuck in the hotel lift' with a young waiter. She's 57 for crying out loud! Fair play!) But I felt a little deflated. Luckily none of my friends had witnessed the 2:00 a.m. showdown between the happy couple, and those of Chris's friends who'd been present were wise enough to keep their mouths shut. So at least I didn't have to deal with trying to laugh it off.

The photos eventually arrived and Chris and I enjoyed picking out the ones we wanted for our album. I sent the proofs to Mum & Dad for them to choose some;

"We don't really want that many darling – we'll never look at them. Just a couple will do nicely." Cheers Mum.

We went to visit Chris's Mum and she, by way of a stark contrast, couldn't get enough of the photos. "Is that all there is, Chrissy?" (Yep – she was allowed to call him Chrissy but no one, and I mean NO ONE else was. On penalty of death).

"I was hoping for some more of the reception. And the dancing. Although you didn't dance together much did you? Sarah you seemed to be having such a lovely time dancing with all your wonderful friends!"

I studied her carefully, looking for a hidden meaning, but there appeared to be none. Chris's mum was sweet and innocent. I didn't have her down as a shit-stirrer and, besides, she had no idea what went on in that room after she'd gone to bed. His sister, Jane, on the other hand, was all-seeing and all-knowing. She had extended her stay from America and was still at her Mum's when we got back from our Honeymoon. I'd had a great chat with Jane at the wedding. I took to her immediately and enjoyed her tales of Chris's childhood antics – she's nearly four years his senior. I'd ventured a question about their Dad but she just gave me a look and said 'Oh, he was a bad one. We were better off without him.' I had tried a couple more questions, but she gave little away. Just commented that she, and to some extent Chris, had seen the way he'd behaved and were determined

42

not to turn out like him. I was puzzled by the way she only sort of included Chris in that sentence, but I didn't query it.

So I was still pretty much in the dark about Chris's Dad as no one would speak to me about him. Was he an axe murderer? A serial womaniser? Maybe 'he' became a 'she'? No idea. One day I hoped to find out.

Anyway, Chris's mum ordered a whole set of the photos and Jane picked out a few that she wanted too. Tea and cake were taken on the lawn and a wonderful day was had by all. Except that, as we were leaving, Jane grabbed me on the pretence of wanting to show me her new jacket. God knows how Chris fell for that one; his sister has no more interest in clothes than I do in nasal hair. Once in her bedroom she said, "Is everything all right? How was the Honeymoon?"

I adjusted my expression from anticipated delight at the new jacket to one of surprise.

"Everything's fine Jane. Honeymoon was great. We just told you all about it."

She pushed the bedroom door to.

"Yes, yes I know. But I heard about what happened at the end of the evening."

I let out an almost cinematic gasp of horror.

"What? What do you mean? What did you hear? How did you-"

"I spent the rest of the night with Dan. You know, Chris's friend? He told me."

Dodgy Dan, of course, was one of the sycophants hanging on to Chris's every word that night and laughing at his wife's humiliation.

Shit.

"Look, it's fine." She leant against the door. "I'm not going to tell anyone. I just want to know how you are. Did it happen again?"

"No!" I said, a little too defensively. "We're good Jane, thanks."

"That's all right then. Only I just want to make sure Chris is not-"

She was interrupted by a shout from her brother: "Sarah! Where are you? We should get going."

"Make sure he's not what, Jane?"

"Nothing. It's fine. You'd better go."

And with that she shovelled me out of her bedroom and into the arms of my husband who was just about to bang on the door.

"It's really lovely Jane!" I managed to stutter. "Just your colour too!"

I was pretty quiet on the journey home. Chris drove and I pretended to be engrossed in a magazine. I wasn't reading a word though. I re-ran my conversation with Jane several times, looking for the true meaning. I couldn't locate it.

"You all right babe? You're very quiet."

"I'm fine darling. Just a bit tired. Actually, to be honest, I'm really getting sick of looking at our wedding photos."

He darted a quick look at me to see if I was being serious and of course noticed my twitching mouth. I never could deliver a wind-up line with a straight face. So we laughed together and all was well with the world once more.

A little later, the realisation hit me that Chris's sister had spent our wedding night with one of his best mates! A tiny involuntary giggle escaped my lips.

"It wasn't *that* funny." Chris said.

"What?"

"Your wedding photos comment."

If only he knew.

CHAPTER ELEVEN

For the next few months or so, life was pretty good. Chris and I worked hard and played hard, embodying the archetypal young advertising executives of the day. A couple of my friends warned me that living together and working together was not a good idea and that we'd get sick of the sight of each other. That didn't happen. We were used to it. We'd worked together from the start of our relationship and we moved in together pretty soon after meeting. So I wasn't really worried about that.

Thinking back now, they weren't really good friends who said that to me. I think they actually *wanted* our relationship to fail. Nice huh? Why are some young women so jealous of other young women? Have they not heard of sisterhood? Women doing it for themselves? (Although personally I always thought that had an entirely different meaning.) Do they never join hands together at Discos and belt out the lyrics to 'I Will Survive" at the tops of their voices?

No, we were good. We were very focused on our work and when we weren't working we were at home cooking together, cosied up at the local cinema or out partying with friends.

What of Chris's promise to me though, I hear you cry. Well call me stupid, dumb, ignorant, pathetic and any other relevant adjective that you care to come up with – but I let him off the hook. We had a chat about it after our Honeymoon and I have to admit I felt sorry for him. I thought he would turn into a different person if he didn't drink (wasn't that the point??) and that I might not like that person so much. So I just made him promise never to drink so much that he became out of control. He jumped on that like a lioness attacking her prey.

"Course I won't darling. I've learned my lesson. I'll never embarrass you again. I promise."

I smiled. A thin smile.

"It can't ever happen again Chris. You know that don't you?"

He took my face in his hands and stared into my eyes. "It won't."

I believed him. Why? Because I wanted to. The alternative didn't bear thinking about.

We did spend a lot of time together, but we also still had our own interests and our own friends. I played squash twice a week and met Becks regularly for nights out. I also kept up my walking and cycling when possible and even managed to persuade Chris to cycle with me in Hyde Park on a few occasions. When I wasn't with him, Chris usually met up with his mates or stayed working late. On most of these evenings he came home. Sure, he was a little worse for wear, but he was coherent and he didn't abuse me. Occasionally he texted to say he was staying at a friend's for the night and although I knew that meant he'd had too much to drink, I managed to put a positive spin on it. He didn't want to come home and risk saying something wrong to me did he? Wasn't that acting in a thoughtful and considerate way? Yes, of course it was. I managed to ignore the fact that he was still drinking a lot.

I drank a lot on occasion too. Usually with my partner in crime, Becky. Generally we just got silly and giggly with our drinking. Occasionally, though, we overdid it and I do recall not making it home after one particularly good night out. Mainly because I was barely capable of standing up. Becks lived the closest to whichever wine bar we were in, so we wisely decided to flag down a cab and retreat to her house for the night. No idea how we managed to come to any kind of decision about anything. Or how we persuaded a taxi driver to let us into his cab. We were actually rolling around on the floor of the taxi, unable to stop laughing. About what, I have no recollection. Undoubtedly to the great relief of the driver, we were outside Becks' place she shared with her boyfriend Ed in no time. Extracting ourselves from the cab wasn't easy though. Eventually we kind of fell out and were greeted by a somewhat bemused Ed who'd been alerted to our arrival by our hysterical giggling. He paid the taxi driver, picked up Becky in his arms and headed up the path, leaving me to follow him in the only way I was able to; crawling like a baby. I do remember the taxi driver's parting words though. 'Good luck with those two, mate – rather you than me!'

I actually had to miss work the next day because I felt so bad. Chris was not amused, but delighted in taking the higher moral ground. He may drink but at least he never missed a day's work from it. Blah, blah, blah. That was some night out though. One which Becks and I relived over and over. But I vowed never to drink that much again in one sitting.

Chapter Twelve

Some six months after our wedding, Mum started to make none-too-discreet enquiries about whether or not I was pregnant.

"I was at Hilary's the other day, Sarah, she had her grandson staying. Oh he's such a sweet little thing! So happy! And you should see the size of him now! Hilary's daughter's younger than you isn't she darling?"

"Yes Mum. She got pregnant while still at school when I was at Uni. Remember?"

A slight pause and a little throat clearing from Mum.

"Oh yes, that's right dear. But he's such a clever little boy! I'd love to have a grandchild to spoil. No chance with your sister now she's gone and divorced that Richard."

"Robert, Mum"

"What love?"

"Caroline's husband was called Robert, not Richard."

"Yes, yes – that's what I meant. Anyway – will we be hearing the patter of tiny feet in your house soon?"

"No Mum."

"Oh. All right, dear. I suppose it's that career of yours is it?"

I switched my phone to the other hand.

"I love my job, Mum and we're in no hurry for children."

And that was the truth. I was only 28 and I felt I had plenty of time yet for babies. Chris agreed – he didn't want children yet either. Or at all, possibly. He'd made a couple of weird comments about not wanting to share me with anyone. I thought at the time that he was referring to a possible threesome and assured him that was not my bag! But in fact he was alluding to us having a baby. I told him that he'd always be my number one and left it at that. I was sure he'd come around to it at some stage – hopefully about the same time that I did.

Not long after the phone call with my Mum, Phil and I managed to land another industry award. And not for Domestos this time, it was for Volkswagen. The most prestigious account we worked on. The most prestigious account that the Agency worked on in fact. Phil and I had worked our butts off on that particular TV script – both the writing of it and the shooting. It was tough but we knew we had a good one in the bag once the edit was complete.

Chris made the announcement to the assembled creative department.

"Listen up everyone, I just got a call. Major leak about this year's Clio Awards. Word has it we're getting one! It's for our VW 'Chasing Cars' commercial and I don't need to tell you who the winning team is; Phil and Sarah again! Congrats guys – well done. Champagne is up for grabs in the games room."

A nice enough announcement, I thought. Some wag who clearly didn't think it through before opening his mouth called out "Your missus again Chris! Isn't it time you won something?!"

Chris shot him a scathing look and I didn't fancy his chances of still being in the Agency's employ by the end of the week.

We had a few drinks and went home. Chris was quiet in the taxi. Oh he'd given me a big hug and said all the right things, but I knew he was sulking. Half of me was cross that he couldn't just be pleased for me, proud of me, but the other half felt sorry for him. He was the Creative Director, the top dog. Unlike some creative heads, he still wrote a few of the Agency ads but had never won an award for a TV ad, either at our Agency or before he joined. You may be wondering how on earth he managed to land a key job without some sort of industry recognition. Well in advertising it was often about whom you'd just taken out to lunch or whom you'd been seen out and about with. If you 'smooched' the right person at the right time, then the job often followed, no questions asked. I wasn't sure whether Chris had in fact sucked up to anyone to get his job; I never asked. I just knew that he was good at it.

I didn't know what to say to him so we travelled in silence.

When we got home, he headed straight for the drinks cabinet and poured himself a large something or other. He didn't offer me anything.

My shoulders tensed; trouble was clearly brewing. Chris was cross. I could have just ignored his ignorance and gone to bed, but I didn't. Why the hell should I? It was my special day and yet again he – my husband, my partner, my soulmate – was behaving like a spoiled child.

I also could have said something like – 'It will be your turn next time Chris, I'm sure of it. It will happen' – but I didn't. He didn't take kindly to me patronising him at the best of times.

So I said nothing and just sat down on the settee and picked up a magazine, feigning – none too expertly I fear – nonchalance.

He remained standing and downed his drink in one. Still I said nothing. I refused to even look at him.

After what felt like an age, he put his glass down, sauntered towards the sofa and sat down next to me. He took my hand and gently turned my head towards him.

"I'm so proud of you babe. I'm sorry…I just find it hard to…"

"It's OK Chris. I understand."

He squeezed my hand more tightly.

"I'm pleased for you, and I'm pleased for the Agency, of course. But the longer I go on without winning anything, without any recognition, the more tenuous my position becomes. I'll lose respect. Accounts maybe. I just don't know what to do."

I stared into his beautiful blue eyes. He was on the verge of crying. I'd never seen him this way before. I always emerged an emotional wreck from any weepy movies we went to see but Chris? Chris was tough as old nails. Nothing much got to him.

I took hold of his other hand.

"You're brilliant at your job. You know instinctively which scripts are good and which are bad. You know whether they'll work or not. You know whether an edit is good or not. You've saved some of our clients from making poor choices that would have wrecked their sales. You're good at what you do darling, you're very good."

"But nothing to show for it! No awards! I noticed that Phil lost a bit of respect for me after you won your first one – what's he going to be like now? He'll be eyeing up my office and measuring it for new carpets and blinds if I'm not careful."

"Phil can't manage people. Hell, Phil can barely manage himself! He's a baby – he needs constant mothering. You know how to speak to people, how to get the best out of them. Sure, you've frightened a few suits and the odd client in your time, but that goes with the job – all part of the fun isn't it? And you're usually right – that's the important thing."

I adjusted my position, kept hold of his hands and waited. Eventually he flopped back into the sofa and let his arms drop by his sides.

"I suppose you're right babe. Thank you. I love you so much. God I'm a twat. I don't deserve you."

I took his face in my hands "You're not a twat. But you're right – you don't deserve me."

He looked at me quizzically, spotted my twitching mouth and smiled. Then he began to tickle me remorselessly. The tickling eventually led to some fairly frenzied (and rather loud) love-making. Not a bad way to end the night I felt, considering the alternative route it could have taken.

CHAPTER THIRTEEN

Looking back on it now, it seemed my life was truly a rollercoaster at that time. A corny observation I know, but it's apt. I suppose, thinking about it, most people's lives are very up and down. It's just not human to be permanently happy and for things to always go our way. I guess in order to fully appreciate the good times you have to have some bad times. But, did the bad times have to be THIS bad?

The Awards Ceremony night arrived and with it, a swarm of butterflies settled in the pit of my stomach. As much as I tried to convince myself that all would be well, I just couldn't relax.

Our table of ten Agency staff was easy to pick out when Chris and I arrived; it was the noisiest. Clearly celebrations had begun early. Phil was there, of course, with Tina from accounts who, amazingly, still hadn't seen through his excessive expenses claims and, even more amazingly, still seemed to find him attractive. The two could be linked, I decided.

"Sarah! Sweetheart! Come and sit next to me! I'll be a rose between two thorns!" Yup, I'm afraid Phil still trotted out the most awful clichés.

I obediently slid into the seat next to Phil, gave him a hug and gave Tina a little wave and a smile. Chris took the only other vacant seat which was directly opposite me, but a long way off as we were seated at a large round table. I tried to indicate to him with some none too subtle eye movement that he should change places with my other neighbour but he either misunderstood my beseeching, or deliberately chose to.

The evening progressed predictably enough. The drink flowed, the food was mediocre and the noise level at our table increased exponentially. Finally it was time for the awards to be given out. There was a huge lot of shouting when our Agency win was announced (mainly from our table I believe) and I somehow managed to hold Phil up as we both went to collect our award. When I returned to my seat, Chris weaved his way over and gave me a big hug and a kiss.

"Well done darling! Isn't my wife wonderful everyone? She's won another sodding award! I can't tell you all how proud I am!"

No one took much notice of him. One or two people smiled in our direction and a couple more came over and clapped me on the back with a 'Well done Sarah!'

I sat stock still. Was I the only person who heard the awful sarcasm in his voice? And did I imagine it or did he squeeze me so hard that he nearly knocked the breath out of me? I was stunned. I looked over at Chris, who'd returned to his seat. I watched as he topped up his wine glass and downed the contents in one. Oh God no, not again. Please God not again.

God wasn't listening though; it happened again. We went home (eventually) and before I'd even got my coat off, he turned on me.

"Think you're so fucking clever don't you, Sarah? Two lovely awards! Aren't you just SO talented!" He slammed the front door behind him. "Who really got those awards for you? Who put you to work on those accounts? Who helped develop your idea for the script? Fucking me, that's who! But do I get anything? Do I get any recognition? No! I fucking don't!"

He banged his fist down hard on the hall table and headed towards the lounge.

"Chris that's just not fair! Why are you being so horrible? Why can't you be happy for —"

"Happy for you? HAPPY FOR YOU? Fuck off you little bitch."

So I did. I hadn't removed my coat, I had my bag in hand and my mobile phone – still a novelty to me then – in the bag. I got out of the house before you could say 'fucking arsehole' and called a taxi. Then I phoned Becky, waking her up of course as it was now about 3:30 a.m., and told her I was on my way over.

Chapter Fourteen

Two hours later, Becky and I were snugly wrapped up in a duvet each, sitting on her couch and talking in hushed tones so as not to wake Ed. We'd as good as finished a bottle of whiskey between us but were still able to conduct a reasonably sensible conversation. I'd gone through the whole events of the night while Becky just listened quietly; hugging me at times, tutting occasionally. At one point she emitted an 'Oh for fuck's sake!' after which we listened intently for a few minutes to see if her loud expletive had awoken Ed. It appeared not

"Never gonna be any good, Sez, he's never gonna be any good. You have to leave."

"I know. I know you're right Becks, but I love him."

She upended the whiskey bottle over her glass to extract the last few drops.

"More fish in the sea, Sarah. Leave him."

"But maybe he can change? If I get him to rehab, we might have a chance?"

"He won't go. He doesn't think he has a problem. You know I like the man, well quite like him, but look what he's doing to you. For God's sake girl, you can't let him treat you this way!"

The conversation went on like this for a while longer until one of us – Becky I think – fell asleep mid-sentence. I soon followed suit and the next thing we knew was Ed waking us up.

"Christ! What the hell are you two doing? When did you get here, Sarah? I'm pretty sure you weren't there when I went to bed."

"Err no Ed, you're right, I wasn't." I opened my eyes cautiously to look at him. "Arrived in the middle of the night – bit of a crisis." Fuck, my head-"

Becks slid out from under her duvet and dutifully fetched us both a glass of water. It was just after 8:00 a.m. and we had to get to work.

"Sod work today," Becks said, pulling the duvet over her again. "That's not going to happen."

I decided I wasn't going in either. Fuck him. Let him stew in his hopefully horrendous hangover. I had enough to contend with battling my own. I rang the Agency and left a message for Phil, telling him I wouldn't be in and that he'd have to carry on the celebrations without me.

After Ed had left for work, Becky and I managed to rouse ourselves with a good shower (or showers rather – one each; much as we liked each other we weren't in the habit of showering together) and some wonderful eggs and bacon. Becks then got serious.

"Right Sez, you're staying here. No arguments. You're not going back to that bastard. You stay here and we'll decide what you'll do. OK?"

"Well…I think I should…"

"No, you shouldn't. You're staying here and that's that. Wait 'til you're sure he's in work and go home and get some stuff. We've only got the sofa for you to sleep on I'm afraid, but it's pretty comfy isn't it?"

I sat down on the arm of said sofa and put my head in my hands.

"I don't know Becks. I don't know if I can do that."

"Look what he's done to you! Think how he's treated you! No no no! You deserve better than this, girl."

Best mates are simply the best aren't they? They tell you what you really know to be the truth but don't always want to hear.

So I crept back to our house in the middle of the day, having established that Chris was at the Agency. He left me several messages on my phone, saying he was sorry for whatever he'd done (seemed the poor boy had suffered a memory lapse again) and please would I 'just come home'.

I couldn't face talking to him so I left a note telling him I was staying with Becky for a few days and that I would be back at work tomorrow.

Tomorrow came and with it a kind of nervous excitement. I was actually looking forward to seeing the bastard – I'd missed him! But I was also a bit scared. I had to stick to my guns. Actually I was more scared of the consequences with Becky if I didn't stick to my guns. But it wasn't going to be easy. Fortunately no one at work knew what had taken place between us at the end of the Awards night; they'd just assumed (correctly as it happens) that I'd had a hangover yesterday which was why I didn't show up to work. Chris, hangover or not, had made it to work but of course didn't allude to anything untoward.

I managed to avoid him for most of the morning before Phil took it upon himself to make an early exit for a lunch date with Tina, thus leaving me alone and very exposed. Sure enough it wasn't long before he showed up.

He closed the door quietly but didn't sit down. He just stood there looking at me with those beautiful pools of blue.

"Sarah, I'm so sorry. I obviously upset you but I don't know what I did."

Didn't he? Really? Or did he just think that everything would be OK if he pretended not to remember?

"Well, Chris, it was the usual. You were jealous of me, you were horrible to me and you told me to Fuck Off." I somehow managed to deliver this with a good deal of insouciance, which I certainly didn't feel.

"Christ, I'm sorry. I don't remember anything. Please forgive me. Please come home."

"No. I'm not coming home until you promise to get some help."

"I'll cut down Sarah, I promise, I'll…"

"Not good enough. You have to get some proper help. And I'm not coming back until I see that you're doing that."

God, Becky was going to be so proud of me!

He hung his head and started to turn away. Then he faced me again and said;

"OK. I'll do it. I'll start going to AA. I promise. So come home. Please."

CHAPTER FIFTEEN

I stayed a couple more nights with Becky, just to make him sweat a little and also to make my point. Becky said I was mad to go back so soon, but I had to. I believed him. He said he had his first AA meeting arranged for next week, and he even told me the exact time and place.

Once we were back together, he was nice, quiet and very respectful and attentive. After a couple of weeks, my doubts got the better of me. I couldn't quite believe it would be that easy. So I followed him after work to one of his meetings. I don't think I'd win any awards for the subtlety of my tailing, but I did get away with it. And do you know he went to where he said he was going and where he said he was going did indeed turn out to be an AA meeting. Either that or a séance. I glimpsed several people sitting around in a circle before I slipped away unseen. I went for a drink by myself to celebrate. No I didn't see the irony at the time.

So, as I said, Chris was nice, he was quiet and he was... boring. I guess I couldn't have everything. He was working hard, putting in long hours in the office and then coming home for dinner, a nice, pleasant chat and then bed. I didn't drink with our dinner as I felt that was just not fair, but I did sneak a whiskey in the evening – which he didn't seem to notice or, if he did, he chose not to say anything.

Becks was frequently on the phone.

"How's it going? What's he doing? Are you OK?"

"Umm – well, he's going to the meetings (she was well impressed with my detective skills), he's not drinking and I'm fine!"

"Really? That's brilliant Sarah. But don't count your chickens, it's early days yet."

Good old Becks, ever the sage.

"But he's boring Becky. He's so…polite! It's like having dinner with a favourite Uncle. And there's no sex!"

"What?? You need to fix that girl, that's not good. Look, just see how it goes – as I said, early days."

So I stuck with it and Chris, it seemed, also stuck with it. I couldn't understand how it appeared to be so easy. The man had gone from drinking a basic minimum of 2 bottles of wine a day to apparently relishing his pint of water with dinner without a care in the world. It didn't seem right; something had to be up. No apparent withdrawal symptoms, no night sweats or thrashing around on the carpet with his tongue hanging out. I did notice his hand shook a bit when he was eating or drinking, but other than that, nada. Was my husband human, I wondered?

I admit that I even donned my raincoat and sunglasses again and followed him another evening, just to make sure he was still going to the meetings. He was. Again, he never spotted me, but I did get some funny looks from passers-by. Probably the sun glasses at 8:00 p.m. on a dark November evening…

I tried to talk to him about everything one dinner time,

but that didn't go down too well. In fact it was the only time that his avuncular mask slipped a little.

"Chris, can we talk? I mean talk properly? Not just about the weather and work and what colour our new lounge carpet should be."

"'Course. What do you want to talk about darling?"

I took a sip of my water.

"Well, I can see that you're clearly making a fantastic effort with the drink, and I appreciate that of course. But…"

I trailed off, not quite sure how to put it.

"But what Sarah?"

Chris had stopped eating and was staring at me intently.

"But you've changed. We used to have fun together and now it's just work, eat and bed. You've become…well, boring."

"Oh dear, I'm so sorry about that darling. I thought this is what you wanted? I'm not drinking am I? What else do you want me to do for you? Stand on my head and sing three verses of 'For he's a Jolly Good Fellow'? For Christ's sake Sarah, give me a break here."

I was tempted to say that I didn't think there were three verses of 'For he's a Jolly Good Fellow', but I stayed quiet. This was dangerous territory.

"I know, Chris," I ventured. "And I appreciate it, really I do. It's just that, is this how our life is going to be from now on?"

"Well you can't have it both ways. Either I drink and we have fun or I don't and we don't. I'm doing this for you, for us."

There was something in the way he spoke that scared the living daylights out of me. It was like he was punishing me. I had made him stop drinking so I had to put up with the consequences, the fallout if you like.

63

Naturally I discussed it in person with The Sage at the earliest opportunity.

"Honestly Becks, you should have seen the look on his face and heard the way he spoke to me. He was kind of smirking and he looked at me in such a nasty way."

"Is there no end to this man's arsenal of weapons against you? He's no good Sez – I wish you'd just effing leave him."

"I can't leave him now, can I? Not now he's stopped drinking for me. That would be too unkind."

"And what's he being to you now if not unkind? He has a problem, and it's a problem that will be with him for life. And therefore with you for life if you stay with him."

"Do you think he's being deliberately boring and withholding sex to get me to change my mind?"

"Wouldn't put it past him."

"Is he expecting me to say; 'oh please start drinking again Chris! Please go back to your old self so that we can have some fun and some orgasms again!"

Becks giggled and almost choked on her wine.

"You don't need a man for orgasms Sarah. I remember us discussing that one drunken evening!"

I smiled at the memory. "Yeah I know, but seriously, do you think that's what this is all about?"

"Like I said, wouldn't be surprised at all. But you are NOT going to give in to him!"

I took a slow slurp of my wine.

"Sarah! Please look me in the eye and tell me you are NOT going to give in to him!"

Becks yanked my face towards hers so fast that we crashed noses and ended up in fits of laughter. As per usual.

"It's OK, Becky," I rubbed my poor little sore nose. "I'm

not going to give in to him. I know that would be stupid. But I've got to do something. Can't carry on like this."

Chapter Sixteen

Well, I did carry on like that. For a few weeks more at least. Nothing changed. Chris was decency and niceness personified. He worked hard, went to his weekly AA meetings, came home for dinner and was boring as fuck. He was fine at the Agency with me, just treated me like everyone else really. The staff must have noticed that he'd stopped drinking, but nobody said a word. Not to me anyway. I don't know what his mates thought – he clearly wasn't going out drinking with them at every available opportunity these days. Every time I tried to talk about how our life had changed he simply shut me up with 'This is what you wanted Sarah.'

But it wasn't what I wanted was it? I wanted the man I loved, the man I married, and the life we shared together but without the shite bits where he was abusive towards me and told me to fuck off. Was that really too much to ask? Most of my friends seemed to be able to manage it. I know they say that you never know what goes on behind closed doors, but I was fairly confident that most of my mates were in pretty good, working relationships.

Take Becky and Ed for example. Couldn't organise a piss up in a brewery between them but they were good together.

You could see they loved each other and they enjoyed each other's company. Actually perhaps they enjoyed each other's company a little too much; I got sick of Becky telling me about their extremely active sex life! Especially as I was going through a bit of a dry period at the time. But my point is that they seemed to just have a normal relationship – you know, the one where you respect each other? I've heard tell of it anyway.

Then one day I had a brainwave. We had to move. That was it, that was the answer to our problems. All of them. Living in London, surrounded by bars, pubs, restaurants and drunks was probably not the best environment for a recovering alcoholic. I put it to Chris one evening, just to break the silence as much as anything.

"Chris, I've been thinking."

He shot me a look but said nothing.

"We need to make some changes. You're working too hard, I'm bored and we don't do anything together anymore except eat dinner. And that's usually in silence."

"But this is what…"

"Don't say it. Please just listen to me. I think we need a change of environment. I'm not talking about our jobs – I think we should move away from London, out into the country. We can get a lovely big house with grounds and maybe horses – you love horses don't you? It could be somewhere commutable. We could get out of London each evening and maybe have some kind of life together again. We could…"

I trailed off, aware that I was probably not selling it that well. Which was ironic, for an award-winning advertising professional.

"What do you think?"

"Spend half my life commuting? No thanks. Good try though."

God he was a fucking bastard.

"We don't need to go too far out. What about Epsom? That wouldn't be too bad a commute to the Agency. And it's great for horses I hear!"

That went down like a lead balloon.

"Look, will you just think about it please? We could have a lovely life away from London. We'll both find new interests, meet new people and maybe…" I paused here before continuing, well aware of the irony of what I was about to say:

"Maybe we could think of starting a family." Although I gave up biology in the third year at school, I was pretty sure that you had to have intercourse in order to get pregnant. Actual intercourse. Not whatever had passed for sex between Chris and I over the last few weeks.

He took a gulp of his water and continued eating. I rambled on, unfazed.

"We have to do something Chris. We CANNOT …" Here I raised my voice a little and paused for dramatic effect. "Continue like this. So please just say you'll think about it. That's all I ask for now."

"I'll think about it."

Said with all the conviction of a serial adulterer professing that he'd think about not being unfaithful again.

CHAPTER SEVENTEEN

Do you know what though, he did think about it. And not only did he think about it, he actually decided that it was a good idea. In fact he eventually got so into the whole thing that he was convinced it was his suggestion to move, not mine! I didn't care. I had my Chris back. He was lively, excited and optimistic. He was still off the booze and still going to his weekly meetings. I was so proud of him.

We got our London apartment valued and were pleased by how much it had appreciated. Houses in commutable areas don't come cheap by any means, but we were surprised by what we were able to afford. Three or four bedrooms, big kitchen, huge garden and a double garage! Our London apartment only had one allocated parking space, so this seemed like a real luxury to us. One of the houses in our price-bracket even boasted its own tennis court!

A great time was had mulling over all of the estate agents' details and picking out the ones we wanted to view. We didn't put our apartment on the market straight away, because we were told it would sell very easily and quickly. We decided to see what was out there for us first before committing to anything.

Since Chris had stopped drinking, our weekends had generally followed the same boring pattern. Chris would work on something in his office at home. I would play squash or go for a cycle and meet a friend for lunch. We'd have dinner together at home and then watch TV or a video for the remainder of the evening, until one of us fell asleep. Usually me. Sunday was sometimes spent with friends – either at their place or ours but never in the pub. We simply didn't go to the pub anymore. At least not together. Occasionally we'd go and see my parents or Chris's Mum on a Sunday. So generally our weekends of late had been pretty predictable and mainly tedious.

Not now though. Now we had houses to view! We booked up three or four for the first Saturday and set off from London with high hopes. Unfortunately, the day didn't start well as we immediately got stuck in a traffic jam. Where on earth was everyone going at 9:00 a.m. on a Saturday morning? Getting the hell out of Dodge I suppose. I could sense Chris's good mood diminishing with every endless minute that we remained stationary. I dug out his favourite Dire Straits album, hoping it would appease him a little. We always sang along to a couple of the songs together, thinking we were God's gift to vocal harmonising. But even though I launched into the first verse, he missed his cue and didn't join in. Spoilsport.

"Don't let this put you off," I shouted above the music. "We're going to be using the train in and out of London mainly, not the car."

Silence. Apart from Mark Knopfler extolling the virtues of free chicks and lamenting his surplus of colour TVs.

"Chris for God's sake! Please!! You've been so looking forward to this. It's going to be OK. OK?"

He nodded begrudgingly.

"Right now, join me on the next chorus will you?"

He did. Finally the traffic jam cleared and we started to make good time. We were due to meet at the estate agent's office before being whisked off to our appointments.

The last viewing of the day was the one. It put a big smile on Chris's face. It was perfect.

He whispered to me on the way out, "Darling, I think we've just seen our future home." Fortunately I agreed. We both wanted the same things for our new beginning. The house had three big bedrooms, one with an en-suite, a further separate bathroom, a good-sized kitchen looking out onto the back garden, three living rooms – the smallest of which would be perfect as a study/office, a double garage and a big garden. At the back of the garden was a large field owned by a local farmer. According to Natalie, our estate agent, said farmer would be happy to consider an offer for renting the field out for horses and stables. That clinched it for us. Chris had always loved horses since he was a little boy and had learned to ride. He told me once that he harboured a dream of having his own horses one day. Where we were going to get the money to buy a horse as well as a house I wasn't quite sure, but little details like that were unimportant at the time.

We immediately made an offer on the house, whilst simultaneously putting our London apartment up for sale. Our offer was turned down. We weren't prepared for that and panicked! I was all for agreeing to the asking price but Chris played it a bit cooler and we eventually settled on a happy medium which suited both us and the sellers. We couldn't believe our luck, although we didn't want to count our chickens too soon. When it comes to house buying and selling it was never over until the fat lady sang. So we remained cautiously optimistic, as they say.

The interest in our apartment was quite incredible. We could have sold it ten times over, probably at a much higher price. We were very happy with what we got though and it wasn't long before we heard the sound of the fat lady doing her vocal warm ups and everything was agreed.

Becky was less happy.

"I didn't think you'd actually move, Sarah. You can't leave me."

"Which part of 'we've decided to sell our apartment and move out of London' did you not understand Becks??"

"Yeah, but I didn't think you'd ACTUALLY do it. You can't go."

"I'll only be a few miles further away; I'm not leaving the country! We'll still meet up as often as we do now. I promise. How long do you think I'd survive without you in my life?"

"Couple of days maybe."

"Exactly. So we'll still meet after work during the week and I can stay with you in London and you and Ed can come and stay with us in the country! We'll go huntin', shootin' and fishin'!"

"Oh good God Sarah no! That's not me at all. Unless you add eatin' and drinkin' to the list!"

"I'm kidding. Eatin' and drinkin' it is."

We laughed together and hugged each other. Our friendship was exceptionally solid. A few extra miles apart would not derail it.

Chapter Eighteen

And so it came to pass that we moved to our beautiful house in the country. We took a week off work to complete the move and to settle in, as there was a fair bit to do. For a start we had a lot of rooms to fill! We spent our time shopping for furniture and choosing new carpets and curtains for the rooms we'd decided to redecorate. The kitchen was perfect and so were the two spare bedrooms. We wanted to put our own stamp on the master bedroom, and a couple of the living rooms definitely needed new carpets. It was a great week, one that clearly stands out in my memory.

We'd lived in Chris's apartment after getting married, so this was our first opportunity to choose things together and to make the home 'our' home. We had so much fun without any cross words or arguments. I really felt that we fell in love all over again during that week. And we had sex! Proper sex! It was fantastic. I was so pleased with myself for having suggested this move. Everything was going to be all right.

You know what they say though? Pride always comes before a fall.

But the fall didn't happen straight away. We went back to work, we got used to the commuting and we adapted to our new lifestyle. I met Becky every Wednesday after work for a night out, and generally made the last train home with seconds to spare. Although I confess I failed on a couple of occasions and ended up on Becks' couch for the night. Chris and I both joined our local squash club where we played most weekends, and we went cycling in the countryside when the weather was good. Sounds idyllic doesn't it? Well, it was. For a good, oh let me see now, four months or so.

Chris had to put the idea of buying his own horse on the back burner. We simply didn't have the funds. Instead, he announced that he was going to join the local Shooting Club. This came as something of a shock to me. What the hell was he going to shoot?

"Don't worry sweetheart, I'm not going to be shooting anything at the moment. I was just chatting to Geoff next door about it and he got me interested. So he's taking me along to the club to see what I think of it."

"OK Chris, whatever. Just don't start shooting animals will you?"

"Course not, love."

I left it at that, happy I suppose that he'd found an interest – and a new friend. I also quite liked Geoff's wife, Lucy, although she was a bit 'horsey' for me. We'd socialised at each other's house a couple of times and we all got on fine. She was never going to replace Becky as my best mate, but she had a sense of humour and she liked a drink so that was good enough in my book.

Turned out that Chris really took to the shooting. So whilst I rushed to meet Becky every Wednesday after work, he caught an early train home and spent his evening with Geoff at the Shooting Club. He never really told me much about his time there, but he was always in a good mood when I returned home, so I was happy. In fact I was usually very happy on a Wednesday evening, having shared a couple of bottles of wine with Becky.

Chris continued to not drink – at least I never saw him drink or drunk. But he had stopped going to his AA meetings which worried me. I thought that was a meeting for life? Rather like the Tesco Bag for Life that you kept on re-using? Apparently not, according to Chris.

"Nope. Not going to those any more. I don't need to. Sarah. I'm fine."

After a few weeks of our new regime though, he started to stay the odd midweek night in London with one of his mates. He said he had a lot of work to do so it wasn't worth coming home late in order to get up and go back to work again the next morning. I went along with it but secretly I was worried that he was back drinking again. I couldn't really say anything though because I had my weekly, boozy night out with Becky and plenty of drink at the weekends too if I wanted it. Well, actually, I could say something and, with the benefit of wonderful hindsight, I should have said something. I wasn't the recovering alcoholic was I? I wasn't the one who turned from sweet Dr Jekyll into the nasty and downright evil Mr Hyde after a few drinks, was I? But I couldn't help it; I still felt guilty for the fact that I could have a drink when I wanted one, but Chris couldn't.

I talked it over with Becky one Wednesday evening, whilst necking back our large quantities of wine, the irony not being lost on me this time.

"I'm worried Chris is drinking again, Becks."

"Oh Christ no! Why? What's happened?"

"Nothing really – I just have my suspicions."

"You mean your woman's instinct. You're probably right. What's he up to? I thought he was doing so well lately that he might even qualify for a Husband of the Year award!"

Becky was still none-too-enamoured with my Chris. I just smiled.

"Yeah he's doing great, but he's started staying in town one night a week and I'm sure he's drinking. He says he's working but when I ask him what he's working on and why he has to stay so late, he's very non-committal and says things like 'what's the matter Sarah? Don't you trust me?' To which I have to reply ''course I do sweetheart!' And then shut the fuck up!"

"OK." Becks thought about this for a while as she slowly sipped her wine. "Well, let's follow him! You were a brilliant snoop back in the day. Let's dust off the old raincoat and sunglasses!"

I looked at her. She was actually serious.

"No, I can't do that, Becky. It's…"

"Why not? You did it before?"

"Yeah, but that was different." I quickly scanned my brain for reasons why it was different before she posed the question.

"How?"

"Umm, well it just was. I simply didn't believe he was going to the AA meetings and had to check."

"Yeah and now you simply don't believe that he's not drinking again, so you've got to check!"

I looked away.

"Well?" she said. "I'm right aren't I? Aren't I always right, Sezzy baby?"

"No, you're not! But yes, you're right."

I was still not entirely convinced it was a good idea but I decided to go along with it. We talked it over and came to the conclusion that it would be better if Becky followed him on her own one evening, assuming he did actually leave the Agency to go drinking. The idea that the two of us could tail him without being seen was just downright amusing. We knew very well that we'd be in fits of giggles before you could say Columbo, our cover well and truly blown.

And so the ruse was set for the following Thursday. When Chris told me that, as usual, he would be staying the night in London with his mate Dan, I managed a pretty nonchalant "OK darling, that's fine. Have a good night." To which he snapped "I'll be working, Sarah, that's all."

Whatever.

I briefly thought about Dodgy Dan and wondered if he'd ever told Chris that he'd spent our wedding night with his sister. Unlikely, I decided. There'd be no way of knowing how Chris would react.

I tapped out a message to Becky: 'You're on Sherlock! For God's sake don't get caught.'

CHAPTER NINETEEN

Turned out Becky was quite the detective. I told her she'd missed her vocation in life. She sat in a coffee shop opposite the Agency's main entrance until she saw Chris emerge at around 6:30 p.m. He was alone. She watched as he hailed a taxi and then ran to flag one down herself, with the immortal words: "follow that cab!"

That cab stopped at a pub in King's Road. Chris got out, paid the driver and entered said pub. At which point Becky could have been a bit stuck. She had to follow him to see who he was meeting and what he was drinking, but surely he'd spot her? Here's where her wiliness really kicked in. She went straight to the Ladies' in the pub and – get this – produced a ginger wig from her bag! When she told me this bit, I was so taken aback that, for a moment, I forgot that my recovering alcoholic husband was in a pub and not at work where he was supposed to be. "Wow Becks," I uttered. "Where d'you get that and whatever made you think to bring it?" "Borrowed it from Ed's sister's place – just thought it might come in handy."

And come in handy it did. With her ginger wig and sporting a pair of glasses to boot, I'd say she was pretty unrecognisable. She did get a few funny looks though, apparently.

Anyway…by the time she emerged from the Ladies', Chris had been joined by Dan. They had a bottle of red wine on the table between them and two glasses. Becks was quite hesitant when she told me this bit on the phone. Ever the optimist, I said, "Chris was just having water from a wine glass though wasn't he? Did you actually see him drink any wine?" She did, of course.

So there it was. My fears were indeed not unfounded. Becks continued to observe them for another hour or so (funnily enough no one hit on her in her ginger wig and slightly oversized glasses) during which time they sank two bottles of wine between them. Her job done, she left, not wishing to see any more.

I was shocked. Yes, I know I'd thought that drinking was exactly what he was doing, but still I was shocked. The lies, the deceit. How to deal with it though? I arranged to meet Becky the next evening for a proper de-brief and to discuss what on earth I should do next.

"Seriously Sarah, I'm so sorry. I was really hoping the little bugger wasn't up to his old tricks. But I saw it with my own eyes."

"I know, Becks. I'm so grateful to you for doing what you did. If it weren't so serious, I'd suggest a night out with us both sporting wigs and specs, just for the fun of it, but…what the fuck do I do?"

"Don't know, girl. Well, I do know, but you won't listen to me."

I looked at her serious face.

"I *do* listen to you. What?"

"You have to leave him, Sez. I've told you. You have to. He's no good. Oh I know he's got beautiful blue eyes and he's sexy as hell but he's a bad 'un and he'll never change."

Shit. She was right of course.

"I don't think I can leave him. I love him."

"I know, but we've had this conversation before. He tried to change but clearly he can't. It's only going to get bad again Sarah."

I thought about our lovely new house. About the week we'd had together buying furniture and new carpets. About the rug in front of the open fire where we'd made love. Our weekend cycle rides together. Could I live without him?

"But how do I handle this? I can't tell him you followed him. He'd have a sodding fit."

"How about you say that a friend of yours saw him in the pub?"

"Umm, not sure. He'd be suspicious about that. He'd ask me which friend and why didn't they come and say hello."

"Look Sarah, just tell him the truth! Why does it matter how you found out? He's the one in the wrong. He's the one who's been lying to you and deceiving you."

"Yeah I know but…oh I'm just not sure I can do that. What would happen then? What would that lead to?"

"Well either he'll apologise and start going to his AA meetings again or he'll lose the plot and try and make you out to be the villain."

"If I were a betting person, I'd go with the latter."

"So then you leave him."

I bit my nails and looked at her.

"OK. I'll do it. I'll tell him the game's up."

But I didn't.

I just couldn't go through with it. All the way home on the train I tried to imagine how I'd say it to him. I conjured up various scenarios in my mind, some of which actually had him apologising to me and telling me how much he loved me. Most though, had him shouting at me and telling me to mind my own sodding business. I must have looked in the depths of despair, because the passenger opposite asked me if I was OK! I smiled sweetly; "I'm fine thank you! Just work problems…you know." He nodded and carried on reading his book. I felt pathetically grateful that someone seemed to be concerned about me and my eyes started to fill up. I quickly looked away. Christ what was happening to me? What had he reduced me to?

So I finally made up my mind that I wouldn't say anything. Because if I did, decisions would surely need to be made. We were happy enough weren't we? It was only one night a week and everything was fine for the other six nights so why upset the apple cart? Of course Becky would be furious, I could hear her voice saying to me 'He's lying to you, Sarah! You can't live with that.'

Well, sorry to disappoint, Becks. But I'd decided I could live with that.

CHAPTER TWENTY

Life was pretty good for a while, once I'd made the conscious decision to ignore the ongoing deception, that is. I think I believed, briefly, that he actually was working late one night a week! Probably because that was what I wanted to believe. After a few weeks though, one night a week sometimes became two nights a week. That was pushing it too far really, but I still decided to remain schtum. Naturally, Becky despaired of me and refused to even discuss the situation. I didn't tell her about the extra night; that would have put a strain on our own relationship, which was the last thing I wanted. Becky was my rock.

As well as staying the odd extra night in town, Chris was also spending more and more time with Geoff at the Shooting Club. I hoped he wasn't drinking on these nights too but reasoned that, even in Chris's book, shooting and drinking don't mix.

One weekend, he announced that he would be going shooting with Geoff on Sunday.

"Sunday? That's a strange day to go to the club isn't it?"

"We're going shooting for real."

I put down my coffee cup.

"What on earth do you mean?"

"I mean, darling, we're going out shooting! Not in the club."

"And what exactly are you going to be shooting?"

"Birds – pheasants, pigeons…you know…"

Well no, I didn't know actually, but I knew I didn't like the sound of it one bit.

"Chris, I hate that. You know I do. You promised you wouldn't do it. Why the hell would you want to kill poor birds?"

"Oh don't be silly, it's just a bit of fun!"

Not for the birds it ain't.

"Well I don't like it. I wish you wouldn't. Can't you just enjoy shooting at the club?"

"I'm going tomorrow, and that's that. Stop telling me what to do for Christ's sake!"

I could have continued but it would have only escalated into an argument. One which I was bound to lose. So I said no more. But I was hugely angry with him. Geoff's wife, Lucy, rang and invited me on a walk that Sunday with her and a couple of friends, and a drink after at the house. I agreed to it, mainly because Lucy wasn't the sort of person you could say no to easily. I would rather have gone out cycling with Chris on Sunday, as was our usual routine.

Lucy's friends were quite nice, but again not 100% my cup of tea…actually maybe not 100% my Pinot Grigio is a better analogy as we drank gallons of the stuff after our walk. One of her friends – I forget their names – became very drunk quite quickly and then very ugly quite quickly. You know the way some women can turn after two glasses of wine? Men too, to be fair, although it usually takes more than a couple of drinks. Well she turned all right. Started slagging off her husband, saying what a useless bastard he was, in all departments it seemed. I barely knew the woman and I really didn't care to hear intimate details of her sex life. Instead I tried to engage Lucy in a conversation about our men and their shooting habits. It was clear that she had no idea what my objection was. It was almost as if she hadn't grasped the fact that they were actually killing birds. Or maybe she just put it out of her head and didn't think about it. All hopes of finding a kindred spirit there were lost anyway. She did tell me though that Chris was borrowing one of Geoff's rifles. *One* of Geoff's rifles?? How many did the man have for fuck's sake? I had no idea that he owned guns, had never seen them anywhere in their house. I assumed they were hiring them from the club. What kind of a neighbourhood had we moved into?

I managed to extricate myself as the friend launched into a fresh attack on her husband and his pathetic attempts at cooking. She didn't even notice me leave, never so much as paused for breath while I lobbed my parting comment at her: "Do your husband a favour – leave him." Lucy heard me all right and shot me a look that was a combination of admiration and admonishment. She accompanied me to the door and whispered:

"Bit harsh, Sarah, but jolly well said girl!"

I toddled back to our house, well pleased with myself.

I wasn't expecting Chris to be home but he was. I could tell immediately that he'd been drinking. He was making himself a sandwich of some sort in the kitchen and had just about every conceivable jar, spread and filling cluttering up the worktop.

"Chris!" The exclamation was out of my mouth before I could stop it. "What on earth are you doing?"

He turned to look at me and automatically switched on his disarming smile.

"Making a sandwich, darling. Want one?"

"Err, no. Thanks. Just eaten." Which wasn't entirely a lie; we'd had some posh nibbles with our copious glasses of Pinot Grigio.

"OK!" He grinned again and turned back to his sandwich making/kitchen destruction.

To say something or not to say something. That was indeed the question. I decided to play it safe at first.

"So…did you have a good time?"

"Brilliant. Fantastic. Haven't enjoyed myself so much in ages."

Cheers Chris.

"And, um, have you been shooting all this time?"

"Mostly yeah – just went to the pub with them all afterwards for a short time."

Aha! I had him now, surely.

"Chris"

"Mmm?" He turned towards me slightly.

"Chris, you've been drinking haven't you?"

"Had a couple, yeah."

Well he'd clearly had more than a couple, but at least he hadn't denied it, so I said nothing. I decided to leave it there and wait till he'd finished making and consuming the sandwich, and hopefully tidying up the bomb site.

I went and sat in the lounge and attempted to feign nonchalance in my usual manner; flicking through a magazine. Unfortunately I'd picked up a copy of Horse &

Hound, which I had no more interest in than I did Stamp Collecting for the Uninitiated, so he undoubtedly saw through my ruse as soon as he entered the room. I did have just enough time to wonder why on earth we had a copy of Horse & Hound in our lounge though.

He sat down in one of the armchairs opposite me.

"Sarah."

I looked up. He had a smear of ketchup just above his lip but I couldn't speak so I just pointed at it and mimed wiping something off my face. He looked totally confused initially but eventually caught on.

"Sarah," he said again, mid-wipe. "Look, it's OK. I just had two drinks and I'm fine! Aren't I?"

"Yes Chris, you're fine. But you seem to have forgotten something. You're not supposed to be drinking. You can't drink. At all."

"But I can! If I can stop at two and feel OK, then it's OK!"

"Is this the first time you've had a drink since stopping?"

"Yes!" His answer was a little too quick and also a little too loud. I knew he was lying of course, but what could I say?

"Really, Chris?"

"Really."

I opened my mouth to contradict him. Now would be the perfect time to disclose Becky's scoop. But still I didn't do it. I simply couldn't face the anger and abuse that would inevitably ensue.

"But now that you've had a drink, surely you'll just start drinking more and fall back into old habits. That cannot happen. I'm not doing that again."

"I know darling, and I promise you it won't happen. I've got it under control. It's all fine."

"Would you go back to the AA meetings again, please?"

"No, I won't." He got up and crossed the room to me. "I said it's fine and that's that." He took my hand, slowly pulled me up, kissed me and then quietly led me upstairs to the bedroom. I obeyed meekly without saying a word. I knew what was coming you see. And I was right. Complete and utter mind-blowing sex, that's what.

Chapter Twenty-one

Over the next couple of weeks, it dawned on me that it was my fault that Chris had slipped back into his old ways.

I hadn't exactly put the glass of wine or pint of beer in his hand, but I had *allowed* it to happen. I had *enabled* him. If I'd confronted him when I first had my suspicions, then maybe he would have stopped there and then. Maybe. I felt consumed with guilt. Completely wound up by the thought that it was all my fault.

Still I didn't tell him that I knew about his nights out in London at the pub, and still they continued. Of course they did. Why wouldn't they? He believed he was getting away with those. God, he must have thought I was stupid. But then again I was, wasn't I? Stupid I mean. I was stupid enough to let an alcoholic start drinking again while I buried my head in the sand.

I thought about telling him what I'd found out on a daily basis. I went over and over what I might say to him and how he might respond. But however much I thought about it, I just couldn't envisage a scenario in my mind where it all ended well and we both lived happily ever after. He would be so angry at my deception that he would surely just start drinking more. At least while he thought he was deceiving me, he was unlikely to push it further than staying a night or two a week in London. So I was doing him (and me) a favour by not telling him. Wasn't I? But then again, dishonesty's not a good basis for a sound marriage, so was I unwittingly ruining our marriage? I was driven demented with all my thoughts. Worse, I couldn't really share them with Becky. She had been very clear about what she thought I should do, and the girl was not for turning. I had no one to talk to and it wasn't doing my mental health any good.

As well as the night or two in London, the Sunday afternoon shooting session (plus pub visit) became a regular feature in our lives. This upset me more than the deception, if I was honest with myself, because it impacted on 'our' time. Lucy regularly asked me round to her place on a Sunday, but I rarely went. Her oversharing friend, it seemed, had very little recollection of that first Sunday, but apparently she'd calmed down a bit regardless and was taking more water with it. Still, I didn't fancy her company much – drunk or relatively sober. I generally chose a cycle by myself or a game of squash at our local club.

Thinking about it now, it really was a shit time in my life. Not quite as shit as getting shot, but still shit. I continued to work hard and loved my job, and I was enjoying the now diminishing time that Chris and I spent together. Outside of that, I was either consumed with guilt or worry – or both – and spent most of my Sundays wondering how much Chris would drink that day and what state he'd be in by the end of it. Mostly he was pretty good. It seemed that he was indeed only having a couple of drinks after the shooting session. I couldn't understand how he could control his drinking in this way. I was under the impression that once an alcoholic fell off the wagon that was it. Back to drinking, daily and endlessly. It was dangerous though because it simply backed up the narrative that I so wanted to believe in, which was that Chris was in control.

I even went so far as to put this notion to Becky over our weekly wine-in. Mistake.

"You believe what you want to believe girl, but you know what I think. The man is an alcoholic. Full stop. He should not be drinking."

"Yes but don't you see, Becks – he IS drinking and he's OK."

"For now. It won't stay like that though."

I actually got a little annoyed with her at this point, which is a rarity.

"Sounds like you *want* him to fail. Why can't you be OK with it if I am?"

"Christ, Sarah! Do you really think I want it to go wrong? Do you really believe I want you to be unhappy? You're my best mate. Why would I want that? I'm just warning you, that's all. I don't think this is going to end well."

"Yeah, I know. Sorry. It's just so difficult not having anyone to talk to about it properly."

"You can always talk to me, you know that. But I may not always say what you want to hear."

I sighed and put my head in my hands.

"It's so hard Becky, it's so fucking hard. I just go over and over everything in my mind, but I can't bring myself to say anything to him. I don't want to spoil what we've got. I love him."

Becky topped up my wine and put an arm around me.

"I know, I know. I don't envy you. God knows Ed's a pain in the arse sometimes but at least he's honest with me and he knows his limit when it comes to drinking. Mostly anyway…"

I smiled. Of course there was a huge difference between getting drunk occasionally (which we all did) and drinking so much that it was ruining your relationship.

"Look, you'll know when the time is right to say something. If you're OK with how things are at the moment, then that's fine. Go with it. But do not let him get away with anything else. If he starts coming home drunk on Sundays or starts staying more nights in town, then you've gotta say something. Deal?"

"Deal."

We clinked glasses and knocked back the last dregs of our wine.

Chapter Twenty-two

A strange thing happened around this time. Or should I say another strange thing as, thinking back, my life was full of weird episodes and occurrences. Chris's sister Jane came home from America for a visit and asked if she could come and stay with us for a few days. She really wanted to see our new house and spend some time with us. I had no problem with this – I liked Jane, although I hardly knew her. Chris seemed strangely perturbed by the proposition.

"She's your sister. What's the problem? You get on OK, don't you?"

"Yeah, yeah I know. It's just the thought of her staying in the house with us."

"Why is that an issue?"

"Oh I don't know Sarah. She's never…I've never… umm…I'll have to…change things around a bit, that's all."

Not like Chris to be so stuck for words. What the fuck? I tried to get to the bottom of his concerns.

"Do you mean it will be odd having her stay with us because she's never actually stayed with you before? Other than at your Mum's place of course."

"Yes, yes – that's it! It will be weird, that's all"

He pounced on my solution a little too smartish.

"It'll be fine, Chris. She's only here for three nights. We can take her out, show her around. It'll be nice. She's your sister, she's family. I wish my sister would show some interest in coming to stay with us!"

"Isn't she on a Kibbutz somewhere? Trying to find herself or something?"

Chris had little patience with Caroline. True, she'd turned a bit weird recently and I hadn't actually seen her for quite a while, but she was still my sister and I harboured hopes that she would one day return to normal.

"Last anyone heard. What I wouldn't give to have Caroline visit though. I miss her."

He had the grace to put his arms around me at this point and I think I almost heard him whisper the word 'sorry' into my hair.

Anyway, we left the Jane issue there and I, for one, looked forward to her visit. She was staying over a weekend, and Chris had agreed to cancel his Sunday shooting date. Maybe that's why he was pissed.

Shortly before she arrived, it occurred to me that I didn't know whether or not Jane was aware that Chris had been going to AA meetings. Probably not, I reasoned. I couldn't exactly see him phoning her up and saying 'hey Jane! Guess what? I've signed up for AA meetings!' I certainly hadn't told her. I wondered if she'd notice that he wasn't drinking.

I have to say that the weekend was a blast. Jane was great company. She regaled us with stories of her work buddies and the highs and lows of life in America. She loved our house and everywhere we took her.

At a restaurant one evening, while she and I were working

93

our way through a particularly nice Merlot, she glanced up at her brother and said "Not drinking Chris?"

"Having a dry month."

"Really?" she said. And I swear the look that passed between them at this point spoke volumes. Unfortunately, I wasn't *au fait* with the language they were using. What did it mean? Jane must know he's an alcoholic, and Chris must know that Jane knows.

These thoughts swirling around in my head did not mix well with the Merlot I was knocking back, and I became ridiculously tipsy and silly. I wanted at all costs to avoid any nasty confrontations. So naturally I started blurting out absolute rubbish.

"Chris has been doing really well at work recently Jane, he's working so hard. Aren't you Chris? He's really licking the Agency into shape! I don't know how I manage to keep my job there – the standard of ads we're producing is ridiculously high! God, maybe it's because I'm married to the Creative Director!"

They both looked at me – with a remarkably similar quizzical expression.

"Goodness I've never realised how much alike you two are! Shall we order coffee?"

"I think that would be an excellent idea." Chris mumbled.

I thought no more of that evening until Jane's last day when we were out for a walk together, just the two of us. After a little small talk and some general chat, she said those few words that had the potential to open up a can of worms.

"So, how's Chris doing?"

"Err…how d'you mean? He's doing fine!" I stuttered.

"I mean is he really having a dry month or what's going on with his drinking?"

I didn't have a clue what she meant. Should I break Chris's trust and mention the 'A' word? What trust? He was lying to me and deceiving me on a regular basis.

"Sarah?"

"Yeah, sorry. Just thinking. I don't really know what to say, Jane. I don't know what you know and what you don't know."

"Let's assume I know everything."

"OK well…then…nope. I still don't know what to say."

Jane stopped and turned to look at me.

"Is he drinking a lot?"

"No, he's not." Was my honest reply.

"Right, that's good. I haven't seen him drink at the house and he didn't drink anything when we were out for our meal the other night. That's odd though, he likes a drink."

Jane giving Einstein a run for his money.

"Yes, well he's cutting down at the moment."

"Why?"

"Because…because…he *was* drinking too much."

There. It was out. Kind of.

"And did that cause problems at work or with the two of you?"

She must have sensed my reluctance to answer.

"Sorry, that's probably too personal. I'm just concerned, that's all. Are you OK? Is everything OK between the two of you?"

I so wanted to open up to this warm and caring person, but she was Chris's sister and I really didn't know her that well. So I didn't, and thereby possibly defined my future.

"We're fine Jane, really. It was a bit sticky (sticky?? Who the fuck was I kidding?!) for a while but he's got it under control and we're OK now."

"Well that's good to hear. I know I'm not exactly on the doorstep, but if you ever need my help with anything, you will contact me won't you? I love my little brother but I couldn't stand by him if he did anything to hurt you."

"Thanks Jane. Appreciate that."

What the hell did she mean? Hurt me? Well he'd hurt me verbally a few times but he'd never do anything to physically harm me. Would he?

Chapter Twenty-three

While all this shit was happening in my personal life, my work life was actually going fairly well. Chris, it seemed, had got over his jealousy of my awards and was treating me well at the office, on top of giving me some great accounts to work on. Around this time, a young male student joined us for some work experience. Chris put him to work with Phil and me. Well, mainly with me, because the lad wanted to be a copywriter. James was 21 and still very wet behind the ears, but I liked him a lot. He wasn't shy, but he wasn't over-confident either and, most importantly, he was willing to learn. We worked together on some TV ads and, after a while, I gave him a couple of radio scripts to have a go at by himself. He did a neat job, as far as I recall. We went to the studio together to record them with our radio producer. James also accompanied me on shoots and edits.

I did spend quite a lot of time with James, but I was his mentor and that's how it works. We got on well and had a laugh together. I remember catching him looking at me a couple of times – you know, looking at me in *that* way – but I just shrugged it off. He was cute, but he was a baby! It was kinda flattering though…

Chris lobbed the odd comment at me about him. 'Enjoying hanging out with your toy boy, are you?' 'How come you were out at the studio for so long this afternoon?' Crap like that. For Christ's sake, he was the one who appointed me as James's mentor!

One time, I stupidly decided to make him a little jealous.

"He's cute, that James, I really like him."

"He seems to really like you. I've seen the way he looks at you."

"Jealous, Chris?" I smirked

Mistake.

"No, I'm not fucking jealous. You can fuck off with him if you want."

I was stunned. What the hell? WAS he jealous? Was he drunk? That was more like it. I had picked a bad moment. It was a Sunday after his shooting/pub session. I hadn't noticed until now, but he'd clearly had more than the usual couple of drinks.

I decided not to pursue it and instead left the room in a calm and sedate manner, which belied my inner disquiet. I went up to our room and lay on the bed. What fresh hell was this? He's drinking more and he's jealous of another man. Boy! I turned everything over in my mind (I was becoming quite the expert at doing that) and decided that the best course of action was to say nothing and to keep James out of our conversations where possible. Yep – you've got it, head-in-the-sand job yet again.

I shouldn't have let him get away with talking to me like that of course but I was worried about what else he might say, or do, if I confronted him.

This was what my life had come to. I couldn't tell my

husband that he was being an arse, that I was only joking and trying to wind him up a little. Neither could I tell him that I wasn't in the slightest bit interested in James, because I loved him – Chris. I could say none of this because he'd probably just laugh in my face or say something hurtful. Or both simultaneously. I was unable to have a normal, rational conversation with my husband, because he was an alcoholic. And what was I doing about that? Absolutely nothing.

I stayed in our room for a while, just to make a point. When I eventually returned downstairs, somewhat cautiously, I was astounded to see Chris walking...no, STAGGERING around the lounge, a glass of what looked like pure whiskey held aloft. Oh dear God. I tried to turn and go back upstairs before he noticed me-

"Sarah!"

I froze on the bottom stair.

"Fuck you doing? Get over here. Wanna talk."

I turned my head marginally "About what?"

"Us! We've gotta start having some fun again!"

"I thought we were having fun," was my weak response.

"Well maybe *you* are with your toy boy, but I'm not the fuck having any fun. I want us to go out more, go to the pub with our friends, stay after work with our mates there for a drink sometimes. What d'you say?"

What do I say? Good fucking question.

"I don't think now's a good time to talk about this, Chris." I climbed up to the second stair.

"Sarah! Get the fuck over here! I said I want to talk!"

I carried on with my ascent of the stairs. "No Chris, I'm not talking to you when you're drunk."

With hindsight, the wrong thing to say.

99

He banged his glass down onto the coffee table and strode over to me in a matter of seconds. I tried to run up the stairs but he grabbed me and pulled me back down. I fell and twisted my ankle, crying out with the pain, but he just dragged me over to the settee and threw me down on it.

"I said I wanted to talk! So we're going to talk, Sarah, whether you like it or not!"

I was terrified. Chris had never been physically violent with me before and I didn't know what he was capable of. Jane's words were spinning around my head 'I couldn't stand by him if he did anything to hurt you.' She knew. She knew he could be like this, but she didn't warn me. Well, actually, I suppose she had kind of warned me.

My ankle was hurting like hell and had started to swell up. I carefully eased myself back on the settee and raised the offending leg, putting a cushion under it. This seemed to have some calming effect on Chris. Briefly anyway.

"Oh Christ, Sarah – did I hurt you?"

"I twisted my ankle when you pulled me down the stairs."

"Well you shouldn't have disobeyed me should you sweetheart?"

I looked up at him, looked into his baby blue eyes, searching for an ounce of sympathy. But they were full of hate. What had I done? Why did he suddenly despise me?

I decided to try and disarm him.

"Could you get me a bag of peas from the freezer please?"

For a minute he looked like he was going to throw something at me, but he turned on his heel and headed to the kitchen.

I wrapped the peas around my painful ankle, which was now the size of a medium to large peach. Chris remained unperturbed. I didn't say anything. What was there to say? Besides, I was frightened of saying the wrong thing. So I just kept schtum.

Meanwhile, Chris had picked up his whiskey again and was pacing 'round the room.

"We've got to do as I say Sarah. We've got to start having more FUN. Christ, my life is so boring. The only fun I have is when I stay up in town with the lads after work and when I go out shooting with Geoff and the boys. Apart from that – boring, boring, boring. You're boring. All you do is talk about work and that fucking toy boy and, oh yes, Becky and your latest escapade with her and oh how funny she is. Boring Sarah. BOOR...RING!"

So there it was. Out in the open. The only time my husband had any fun was when he was drinking. He didn't enjoy his work, he didn't enjoy his lovely house, and he clearly didn't enjoy me anymore. Where the hell did we go from here?

"I'm sorry you feel that way, Chris," I ventured. "I had no idea you were so unhappy."

I couldn't mention the drinking, clearly.

"Yes I'm sodding unhappy, and it's all your fault. You stopped me from drinking. I'm nothing when I don't drink. I need to drink, Sarah. And you're not going to stop me anymore."

I'd done a great job of stopping him to date, hadn't I?

I felt so vulnerable, lying there on the settee with a pack of peas wrapped around my increasingly swelling ankle. I was in no position to take on a drunken, rampaging Chris.

"Chris..." I looked up into his face, beseeching him. "Chris, please, I'm in a lot of pain. Could we talk about this later?"

101

Could have gone either way. Luckily for me, it went the right way. His expression softened a bit as he put down his drink. He then knelt (or kind of fell) on the floor next to me and took my face in his hands.

"Sarah. Darling Sarah. I love you. I'm sorry. Yeah, we'll talk later but things have to change. I can't stand living like this."

I couldn't stand much more of his whisky-soaked breath in my face, so I was relieved when he let go of my head and staggered back up to his feet. He retrieved his drink and made his unsteady way out onto the patio, sitting down heavily on one of the chairs. I decided to make good my escape and somehow managed to hobble upstairs to the bedroom, where I lay on our bed with a throbbing ankle and a bag of now not-so-frozen peas. I wondered briefly how I was going to navigate public transport to get to work the next day and decided to phone Becky to off-load. And to get her advice, though I could pretty much guess what The Sage had in store for me.

CHAPTER TWENTY-FOUR

Becky, of course, remembered our last conversation on the subject. The one where I agreed to say something if things got out of hand. I tried questioning whether this constituted 'out of hand', but that turned out to be the wrong way to go.

"You just told me that he manhandled you down the stairs and threw you onto the settee. Hurting your ankle in the process. I'd call that fucking out of hand all right."

"It was only a couple of stairs."

"He hurt you! He shouted at you! He called you 'boring'! Didn't you just say all that to me?"

"Yeah, but …"

"Yeah but nothing," Becky cut me off. "I'd like to come over there right now and give him a piece of my mind. How dare he Sarah? How bloody dare he?"

She paused for my response. But I said nothing.

"Sarah, you have to realise that he's crossed the line here. I'll say it again – we talked about this and you said you would do something if things got worse. Well they just got worse. So what are you going to do?"

"I don't know. I also don't know how I'm going to get to

work tomorrow; my ankle is the size of a melon and it hurts like hell."

"OK. First things first. Call you neighbour – the posh cow – Lucy isn't it? And get her to take you to A&E. Just tell her you fell down the stairs and Chris can't drive you cos he's had a drink. Get your ankle sorted, Sez."

"OK. I'll do that."

"Then, we'll talk. We'll make a plan. So call me when you're home from the hospital. OK?"

"OK Becks. Love you."

"Love you too, you silly fool. I've got your back."

Thank God somebody had.

Lucy, as it turned out, had also been drinking. She slurred an apology on the phone, saying she was in no fit state to drive me anywhere. She then shouted to her husband Geoff, but forgot to move her mouth away from the phone to do so, and I got the full blast of it. Geoff's surely not going to be any use to me either, I thought, not if he's anything like the state Chris is in. But a very sober Geoff arrived on the phone saying of course he'd drive me to the hospital.

"But Geoff…" I wasn't sure how to put this. "Umm, haven't you had a drink too? You know, with Chris after your shooting shenanigans?"

"On sodding antibiotics Sarah, can't drink for a few days. I'll be 'round in two minutes."

I managed to make my way downstairs, grab my handbag and a jacket and head out of the front door without Chris seeing me. I would text him later from the hospital. Not because he would be concerned about where I was, I reasoned, but in case he decided to go on a rampage around the house when he couldn't find me.

Geoff pulled up in his none-too-subtle bright blue BMW and I eased myself into the front seat, immediately relaxing into the soft leather upholstery. Christ! Whatever did this car cost? I didn't even know they made cars this plush. I turned to Geoff after doing up my seatbelt.

"Thanks so much Geoff – really good of you. Sorry to put you out."

"No problem at all. What happened? Lucy said you fell down the stairs?"

"Yeah. Bloody stupid! I was puzzling over something on my new phone coming down the stairs, and I missed the last one. Really hurts."

"Looks pretty swollen all right. Move the seat back and tilt it a bit, might help. You need to keep it raised."

I did as I was told, feeling more like I was relaxing on a beach somewhere rather than reclining in a car. Although full relaxation wasn't really possible with a throbbing, swollen ankle.

"Hope Chris helped you, did he? Good job he was home."

"Err, yeah. Good job. He helped a bit."

Geoff shot me a sideways look but said nothing.

We travelled on in silence for a couple of minutes until Geoff said something to me which my mind simply refused to compute.

"Has Chris selected his gun yet?"

Nothing to say to that.

Geoff looked at me "You asleep, Sarah? Did you hear what I said?"

"Not asleep, no. Just…what do you mean 'Has Chris selected his gun yet?'"

"Didn't he tell you? God, I probably shouldn't have said

anything. He was looking at getting his own rifle for shooting. He borrows one of mine, which is fine of course, but he said he wanted to get his own."

"Right. Umm… no. He didn't tell me that."

"Best say nothing, Sarah – he'll surprise you one day no doubt!"

Oh yes. Some fucking surprise that would have been. Jesus Christ.

"Where do you keep your guns? I've never seen them when I've been at your house."

"Keep them locked up in a cabinet in the drawing room. Perfectly safe. I'm the only one who has a key."

Who the hell has a drawing room in their house these days? Sounded like something out of Cluedo.

We continued in silence again for a couple of miles, whilst I tried to digest this fresh hell. Guns I hated. Killing animals I hated. Chris killing animals with guns I definitely hated. And one thing I knew for sure; guns and alcohol rarely go well together.

Chapter Twenty-five

Knowing I'd be in for a fairly long wait in A&E, I dismissed Geoff and told him I'd get a taxi home.

"I'll call in on Chris and let him know how you are."

"No! I mean, umm, no don't worry Geoff – I'll call him. You've done enough. Thanks again."

No reply came in from Chris, so I didn't know if he'd even read my text. Didn't care either.

I had plenty of time to think – although an A&E waiting room is not the ideal place in which to do your best thinking. I tried to shut out the cries of a child who appeared to have shut his fingers in a door. Or more likely he'd had his fingers shut in a door, I doubt it was self-inflicted. I also tried not to gag every time a nearby youth threw up in his 'sick bowl'.

So what was I going to do? I went over the events of the evening in my mind, remembering what Chris had said to me and how, at one point, he'd looked at me with so much hate in his eyes. But then he'd said he loved me and that he was sorry. Been there before though Sarah, remember? And the gun! He deliberately hadn't mentioned that to me because he knew I wouldn't like it. So what was he going to do? Hide it somewhere? Not tell me? Or spring a lovely surprise on me? I was so angry and confused and hurt. And in pain.

Eventually I was examined, given an x-ray, bandaged up and sent on my way with a walking stick and instructions to keep my sprained ankle elevated as much as possible for the next three or four weeks. Yes I could go to work, but had to keep the leg up.

In the taxi on the way home, I rang Becky again. I told her about the gun and I told her I wanted out.

"Yes!!!" she shouted. So loudly that even the taxi driver heard her and gave me a quizzical look via the rear-view mirror. "Finally. You're doing the right thing, girl. I've been so worried about you. Ed and I will drive over and get you. OK?"

"No Becky, don't do that. Chris will only cause a scene. That'd be awful. I'll get a taxi to the train station and then maybe you could pick me up the other end?"

"How will you manage with your leg though?"

"I'll be fine. They've given me a shitload of painkillers and I can walk OK with the stick. I'll text you later."

When we arrived at the house, I decided to pay off the driver and order another taxi when I needed it. I concluded that it might take me quite a while to navigate the stairs and get my stuff together.

Chris was sitting in the lounge when I walked in. He didn't get up but turned to look at me. His face was full of concern. And, weirdly, he appeared pretty sober. How come he'd sobered up so quickly? I suppose I had been gone several hours so it was possible.

I didn't want to engage him in conversation so I headed for the stairs. He, however, wanted to talk. Of course he did.

"How are you, Sarah? What did they say?"

"Sprained ankle, that's all."

"Right. Does it still hurt? Are you OK?"

What a loaded question that was. I looked at him, undecided about what to say.

"Doesn't hurt at the moment no. But no, I'm not OK. I'm going to Becky's."

I started up the stairs, in a sort of *déjà vu* scene. He came up behind me and I froze.

"Sarah, I'm so sorry. I'm such a shit. I didn't mean to hurt you. I hate that I hurt you."

"We've been here before Chris, several times. Only this is the worst. I can't handle it anymore. I'm going to Becky's."

"You can't go like that! How are you going to get there?"

"Taxi, train, then she'll pick me up."

"Sarah, please don't go. Please don't leave me. I need you. I love you. I won't do this again, I promise."

I wavered. I almost fell for it. But I didn't. Becky would kill me if I went back on my word. And she would be right. Enough was enough.

"I'm going, Chris."

Chapter Twenty-six

Becky's sofa was more uncomfortable than I remembered it being the last time I'd crashed there. But it was somewhere safe to lay my head and I was grateful for that. They were so kind, Becky and Ed. A bottle of wine and takeaway pizzas appeared soon after we arrived back at their place. I was ravenous and tucked into the pizza but held off on the wine. Becky was concerned.

"It's 'cos of all the drugs, Becks – better not mix them with alcohol." Common sense of course, but it came as something of a surprise to me that I was capable of that, and it didn't cut it with Becky.

"OK, if you say so. But if I don't see you necking back some booze tomorrow night, I'll be very worried."

Good old Becks.

I really didn't want to face Chris at work the next day – or the next week or month for that matter – so I texted him to say that as it was difficult for me to travel with my sprained ankle, I would be working from Becky's place for the week. I'd liaise with Phil and also the creative secretary. Of course I actually should have been *asking* him if it was OK for me to work from Becky's, rather than telling him that's what I was doing. He was still my boss after all. But sod that; he'd manhandled me down the fucking stairs and I'd ended up in A&E. He really didn't have a leg to stand on. Which made two of us.

I wasn't expecting a reply, but I got one. It was a very sweet and kind reply, telling me to take my time, look after myself and not to worry too much about work. Oh yes, and he was missing me and wanted me home.

Ignored it.

Becky couldn't stop going on about how brilliant it was that I'd finally left him and what a bastard he was. She kept telling me that I'd done the right thing and that I was very brave. But the more she went on, the more I missed Chris. Becky had never really hidden the fact that she didn't much care for him. It's tough when your best mate doesn't like your husband, and vice versa. The two people you love most in your life – you want them to get on don't you? But it's not a given so you just have to deal with it if the love ain't there.

How true it is though that when somebody slags off one of your nearest and dearest, you start to feel defensive. If only Becky knew she was playing it all wrong. I listened to her and didn't say much, but as she came out with more and more negative shit about Chris, my feelings towards him softened.

It must have suddenly dawned on her that she was being too dismissive about him, because she swiftly started retracting her comments and apologising.

"Oh God Sarah, I'm sorry. I'm ranting too much aren't I? He's your husband of course and you love him. I shouldn't have said all those things about him. I'm just so angry at the hurt he's caused you over the years, and now this!" She gesticulated wildly at my bandaged leg, spilling some of her wine over it in the process. She didn't notice.

"You deserve better, really you do. I'm sorry – it's just that I care about you. You know that, don't you?"

"'Course I do Becky. It's OK. I know how hard it is for you to watch all this happening. I just don't know what to do. Every time I think of leaving him I get this hollow feeling in my gut. It's hard to describe."

"What do you mean 'think of leaving him'? You have left him haven't you?"

"I have for now yes, but…" There it was again, the doubt. I really didn't believe that I had, or could ever, leave Chris permanently.

Becky knew better than to go on about it anymore. She gave me a hug and said that I was welcome to stay with them as long as I wanted and that I just had to promise to think everything through very carefully, and not to forget about all the hurt he'd rained down on me.

I promised.

I stayed with them a week and worked from the flat. Well, sort of worked. Watched a fair bit of daytime TV too, which was pretty eye-opening. How did people who regularly watched daytime TV sustain the will to live? I kept my leg propped up as much as possible and soon noticed that the swelling was beginning to go down. I still had to pop the occasional pain killer but decided that alcohol probably provided the best relief of all, so I self-medicated with that. Only in the evenings of course, and in the company of Becky and Ed; I wasn't about to start drinking alone.

It was interesting to observe how another couple interacted with each other. I noticed how relaxed Becky and Ed were in each other's company. They were totally themselves and at ease, and had very few arguments. Oh,

Becky moaned a bit to me about how lazy Ed was at times and how she had to give him a kick up the backside every now and then to do anything round the flat, but, if I'm honest, Becky wasn't much different. Obviously she couldn't see that though and I refrained from pointing it out. Ed was so nice to her; he listened when she spoke, didn't interrupt her and didn't say any unkind things. Even when she rabbited on and he couldn't get in a word edgeways. And she was lovely back at him too.

What they had for each other was not only love, but respect. It reminded me of something I'd once read, which was that to truly love someone you had to also respect them. Did Chris respect me? It didn't feel like it a lot of the time. Seeing Ed and Becky together made me realise that I wasn't always my true self with Chris. Surely that was wrong? What was I afraid of? That he wouldn't like my true self? Or that if I didn't put on a bit of an act when required that I might upset him and he'd shout at me or be horrible to me? I felt that I was treading on eggshells at times. But, I reasoned, those times were only when he was drinking. When he wasn't drinking, he was lovely and we had a great relationship. I tried to ignore the little voice telling me that he was bored and also boring when he didn't drink. Seems he needed alcohol to be the person he thought he was meant to be. But did I want to spend the rest of my life with that person? No, I did not. Could not. I was sensible enough to realise that. The drinking had to stop and, once he'd conquered it, we'd find new happiness together and he would start enjoying life again.

That was it. Sorted. Clearly I had a fair bit of time for thinking, in between coming up with potentially award-winning ad campaigns, watching daytime TV, chatting with Becky and Ed and administering my liquid pain relief.

During the week, I got regular texts from Chris saying how much he missed me, how sorry he was and asking when was I coming home. I sent him just the one reply, which read 'not sure.' I didn't want to get into a battle of texts. Partly because it took so long to type the bloody things. I was still getting to grips with my new-fangled mobile phone. He called me several times too, but I didn't answer. Equally I didn't want to get into discussing our future over the phone.

Instead I came up with a cunning plan. Towards the end of the week, I sent Chris a text saying I'd like to meet him in a café near work at 5:00 p.m. on Friday. I wondered briefly if he'd be able to get away from the Agency at that time, but he agreed with alacrity.

Chapter Twenty-seven

He was there ahead of me and jumped up to help as I struggled in with my bags and the walking stick. He couldn't suppress a smile when he noticed I had my overnight (or rather over-week) bag with me. Clearly he thought he was home and dry. Little did he know what was coming though.

"Sarah." He gave me a big hug and took my case from me. "It's so good to see you. I've missed you. How are you?"

I took my seat without a word and tried to catch the eye of one of the flitting waitresses. Failed miserably, always do. Chris, of course, had no trouble attracting their attention.

"Latte, darling? Anything to eat?"

"Just a latte, thanks." He ordered two.

We sat in silence for a while, his beautiful pools of blue beseeching me to say something. For God's sake, why did he have to have such beautiful eyes? I refused to look at him until our drinks arrived.

Fortified by a few slurps of coffee, I finally let him have my ultimatum. The one I'd practised over and over in my head and, yes, out loud too.

"Chris, if you want us to be a couple again then things are going to have to change. You know that, right?" I risked a look into his eyes, and quickly glanced away again before the spell took hold.

"OK. What are you saying here, Sarah?"

"You have to start going to AA again and we need some counselling sessions together." There, it was out. My hand shook as I took another sip of my latte.

He said nothing. I suppose he was weighing up his options. Option A: I get the love of my life back but I can't drink; Option B: I lose the love of my life but I can carry on drinking until the cows come home. Tough choice I suppose. Depends which you love more; your wife or alcohol. I fixed my eyes on the table and waited to find out.

"That's a difficult one, Sarah."

"Is it?" I slowly raised my head and glared at him. "Is it really?"

"No, I mean, it's not *that* difficult – I want you back of course. And the therapy stuff is fine. But no drinking? That's tough."

I sighed.

"You must surely know by now that your drinking is ruining our relationship. If you could only restrict it and learn to say no when you've had enough, we'd be fine. But you have to face it, Chris – you're an alcoholic. An addict. You need help."

"But my life is so boring when I don't drink. Could I try cutting down? Would you come back and we try that?"

I stared at the remnants of my coffee.

"No. We've tried that Chris. I can't take any more of your drunken abuse."

"Becky's been filling your head with stuff I see. Typical."

I banged my fist down on the table, causing a few heads

to turn our way. I was so angry. I counted to ten before replying to him.

"I do not need Becky to tell me that I shouldn't put up with your abuse. Becky has been a good, supportive friend. She's been a shoulder to cry on, someone to talk to. And God knows I've needed that. Have you any idea how much you hurt me when you go on your drunken sprees?" I kept my voice low, even though the temptation to shout at him was huge.

He looked a bit uncomfortable. "Yes. I know I've hurt you Sarah. And I've said I'm sorry. I won't let it happen again."

"Heard it all before, Chris! The apologies, the 'I won't do it again' stuff. I'm surprising myself a little here, as well as surprising you no doubt, but I am not coming back unless you agree to my terms. So what's it going to be?"

He looked at me for a moment.

"Absolutely. Of course I agree. I love you and I want you back home with me. It's not going to be easy though."

He looked crestfallen. My heart melted.

"Oh Chris," I took hold of his hand. "I know it's not going to be easy. But you've done it before so you can do it again. I'll help you. I won't drink around you and we'll start doing more things together, having fun together. Right?"

Part of me noticed that he'd pretty much switched off from what I was saying, but I pressed on regardless.

"We'll…um…we'll book a holiday! How about that? We haven't been away since our Honeymoon. We'll go cycling together! And, maybe Chris, we could think about having a baby?"

That brought him back to planet Sarah all right.

"Christ, one thing at a time, woman. So are you coming home with me now? Or did you just bring the case for show?"

"Not so fast Mr Hobson. I will come back with you, yes, but you have to contact the AA now, before we go."

"Have you done something to the car, Mrs Hobson? Do we need to call them out?"

I looked blank for second but soon caught on.

"Ha ha – nice one! But you don't get away with it that easily. You still have the number for your sponsor right?"

He nodded.

Phew! That was a gamble; I actually thought he'd deleted it.

"So call him and tell him you want to start coming to the meetings again."

Where the hell was all this strength coming from? I hardly recognised myself. Again I thought how proud Becks would be of me. But I was fighting for my marriage here, a marriage I very much still wanted to be one half of. I just hoped that Chris felt as strongly about it as I did.

Meek as a child, Chris took out his phone and scrolled through his contacts. I felt awful but couldn't stop myself leaning in as he spoke, just to make sure he was actually speaking to Mike. He was. He arranged to go to the next meeting, which was on Wednesday evening.

He ended the call and looked at me.

"Done. Now let's go. I can't wait to get you into bed – even if I have to carry you up the stairs with that ridiculous bandage you're sporting."

"Oh." I said.

"Oh what?"

"My Doctor said sex was out for a couple of weeks."

"What?? You've sprained your ankle Sarah, not your sodding vagina."

"Yeah, I know but …" I looked up at him and grinned.

"I'm kidding Chris!"

"Oh thank God! Come here."

He helped me up and gave me a big hug. We headed slowly to the station, to begin the next phase of our marriage. Which, alas, turned out to be relatively short-lived.

CHAPTER TWENTY-EIGHT

Counselling sure was an eye-opener. I found someone local whom we could go to in the evening, after work. Better than going to a place in London, I figured; we'd be rumbled by a work colleague or a friend in no time. I wanted this to be just between the two of us. Well the two of us, and Becky, of course.

The first session was like the Spanish Inquisition. So many questions, most of which I felt I knew the answer to, but as the probing deepened I began to wonder if I really knew myself or my husband at all. Have you ever tried asking a therapist a question? Don't bother. It gets turned around into ANOTHER question and fired back at you. 'Why do YOU think he likes to drink so much?' That sort of thing. At one point I answered one of her questions with 'I don't know, you're supposed to be the bloody expert here.' This prompted a smirk from Chris and we shared a lovely intimate and conspiratorial moment, smiling at each other.

I'd never thought that Chris's calling in life may well have been in the world of acting, but these sessions revealed a hitherto unknown talent to me. He put on the performance of his life. I think even our counsellor was taken in, although surely she was trained to spot the difference between the truth and outright make-believe? She of course tried to probe Chris about his childhood and upbringing, but he was not very forthcoming. Simply said his Dad had never been part of his life much and that he'd had a happy childhood with his Mum and sister. He deflected any further attempts to discuss his relationship with his Dad. The counsellor and I both knew there was something more to hear there (OK, so maybe he wasn't destined to be an actor after all) but short of waterboarding him it was clear we weren't going to get anything more out of the man.

I, by way of a distinct contrast, was like an open book. I went into the sessions thinking; OK this is all about Chris. It's about Chris and his addiction and how we're going to deal with it. I wasn't expecting the spotlight to be shone on me quite so much. Turns out I had a fair few problems that I didn't know about! My childhood wasn't quite as happy as I thought it had been, my self-esteem was lower than it should be. Also – who knew – I saw what I wanted to see in life and often ignored or glossed over the elephant in the room, preferring my own narrative to the one that was plainly being played out before my very eyes. I was the one who ended up crying in most of the early sessions, not Chris. Chris? Well he was Mr Cool, Mr Nonchalant, Mr Nothing-to-see-here. Bloody hell!!

That said, we did actually get a kick out of going to the sessions and they somehow brought us closer together. We always went out for a meal afterwards, generally to our favourite local Italian. We'd go over everything and laugh a lot. That was great of course, but it soon dawned on me that Chris wasn't exactly taking the counselling seriously, and surely the point was for him to take it very seriously. To learn something from it and to make and accept changes in his life.

He was going to the AA meetings regularly though. Well, at least I think he was. Short of tailing him again I couldn't actually be sure of course. But I wanted to believe he was, so I did. The counselling clearly wasn't working on me either...

I did ask him once if I could come to a meeting with him, thinking this might help me understand the disease a bit more. He explained, though, that the meetings were 'closed', meaning they were only for alcoholics. Family and friends weren't permitted. It was the first time he'd referred to himself as an alcoholic. Although I'm not sure that was his intention.

He had stopped staying up in London during the week, but he did still go shooting on Sundays with Geoff and the gang. I couldn't ask him to give that up; the man had to have some enjoyment in life (aside from his work and his wonderful wife, of course). I monitored him carefully each time he came home on a Sunday, but there was never any sign of drink on him. As I did the last time he gave up drinking, I wondered how he could do it with such apparent ease. Addicts were supposed to suffer weren't they? Withdrawal symptoms and all that. I never saw any signs of those. Oh he was a little more muted and a little less fun of course, like the previous attempt, but he seemed to function perfectly well without the booze.

We started doing more things together at the weekends and a couple of nights during the week after work, and he really seemed OK to me. Head in the sand? Was I missing something? Writing my own narrative as per?

Becky was on the phone to me fairly regularly, plus we met up once a week still.

"So? How's it going?"

"Good. Good. Maybe too good?"

"What d'you mean?"

"I don't know. On the face of it he's doing well. He's going to the meetings – at least as far as I can tell – and we're doing the counselling. He appears to be fine. But it seems too good to be true."

"Well you've been here before Sarah, so maybe it *is* all too good to be true. But you've got to stick with it – still early days. How's the counselling going?"

"I'm learning more about myself than I am about him! But it's good I think. There's definitely something he's hiding about his relationship with his Dad though. The counsellor knows it and keeps trying to get it out of him but he's not saying."

"What do you think it is?"

"Don't know, but Jane hinted at something there."

"Why don't you get in touch and ask her?"

"Just don't know her that well. I've only met her a couple of times."

"Are you happy, Sarah? Are you able to have a drink yourself sometimes? You have to be able to do that, for God's sake. You're not an alcoholic, remember, you're a regular person who needs a drink every now and then!"

"I am happy, I think, yeah. It's hard because a bit of the fun goes out of Chris when he's off the drink altogether. But then I'm not living on a knife-edge, wondering when he's going to turn up drunk and start abusing me or throwing me down the stairs. We're doing a lot more stuff together and he's working hard, so I guess we'll just have to take it a day at a time and hope that this soon becomes normal for him. And yeah – I do drink but not in front of him. Told him I wouldn't do that."

"Well that's good. Sounds like it's going in the right direction. Hang in there, Sez; if this is what you want then you have to keep fighting for it. But remember, I'm always here if you need me."

"Where would I be without you, Becky? You're the best. Love you loads."

CHAPTER TWENTY-NINE

Remember the rifle that Geoff had asked me about? The one Chris was intending to buy? Well, in the euphoria of getting our life back on some sort of track, I had forgotten all about that particular gem of information I'd been inadvertently handed. Forgot all about it that is until I came home from a squash game one Saturday afternoon to find Chris in the living room surrounded by bits of what appeared to be a metallic puzzle. He had a cloth in his hand and was madly polishing one of said bits.

"Chris!" I shouted. "What on earth are you doing?"

"Hmm? Oh hi Sarah. Just polishing my rifle."

As you do. On a Saturday afternoon. In your living room. In suburbia. Without actually informing your wife that you've bought a rifle.

I sat down on the nearest armchair, not quite sure what to say or how to handle this. Chris continued to polish away without so much as a glance my way.

"Chris, why…what are you doing with that in here?"

He sighed and carefully laid the offending object down on the table. Which at least he'd had the foresight to cover with newspaper.

"I bought an air rifle. I don't want to keep borrowing Geoff's. It's nothing to get all worried about, it's just a rifle for my Sunday shootings."

Nothing to get all worried about, the man said. Firstly, he knew how much I hated him shooting anything living, secondly, it's quite a different thing owning a gun from borrowing your mate's, and thirdly, he didn't bother to bloody ask me!

"Don't you think we should have discussed this first Chris?"

"No." He looked across at me. "Why would we do that? I'm the one who goes shooting, not you."

"Yes, but – it's *our* house. You know I hate you shooting anyway, and now you've brought one of those horrible things into our house."

"I'm well aware you don't like it, but that's just hard luck – I *do* like it. Nothing's changed. I've been going shooting with Geoff and the boys for a long time now. What's the big deal here?"

"The big deal is that you've brought a gun into our house. I don't want a gun in the house. Where are you going to keep it anyway? Am I going to have to look at it every day?"

"It will be kept under lock and key in a special cabinet in my office. You won't have to look at it at all."

I got up and started pacing the room. I didn't like this. I didn't like it one bit.

"I thought we were going to start doing more things together, not apart. Now that you've got your own *killing machine* are you going to start going out shooting more?"

"Dunno. Probably not. I enjoy Sundays with the lads, that's all. But if I decide to do more, that's up to me isn't it? Not you."

I knew I was on dangerous ground here but I kept pushing.

"Chris, I'm really not happy about this."

He stood up quickly, bashing his knee on the table in the process.

"Ow! Fuck!" He started hopping around the room. "I don't care if you're fucking happy about it or not! You've taken away one of my main enjoyments in life, you're not taking away another one!"

OK that was a bit below the belt, but I guess I deserved it in some way. But ...no, that just wasn't fair. I didn't deserve it.

"Taken away your drinking? You make it sound like I'm the one who controls that. I'm not – you are. You agreed to it, remember? You agreed to it because it was either that or I walked! Remember that too? Are you regretting your decision?" I continued pacing the room. Boy was I angry now.

"Yes I regret it! I regret it every single bloody day! But what can I do? I don't want to lose you and you gave me no choice. So I'm trying to get on with my life and enjoy it as best I can without drinking. But Sarah, you have to let me do the other things I want to do. You can't take everything away from me."

I sat down again. He was right, I 'spose. He had given up the drink and he was trying his best at a life without it. Was I asking too much of the man?

"OK, Chris. OK. I understand. I don't like it but you're right. I can't stop you from doing it. Just please make sure you keep that bloody thing locked up when you're not using it. It frightens me."

"I will, Sarah. Do you think I'm stupid?"

Well, with the benefit of hindsight...

Chapter Thirty

So we got over another hurdle in the seemingly unending obstacle course that was our marriage. How many more to go I wondered? Hurdles I mean. Is marriage really supposed to be this difficult? The ones you read about or saw played out in films appeared to be mainly pretty solid. Well, apart from real Hollywood marriages that is, they didn't seem to last much longer than a sneeze. I didn't have experience of many real-life ones with which I could compare ours. My sister's ended rather unceremoniously after less than two years. Mind you, she had good reason. Her husband was a twat of the highest order. Mum and Dad's marriage seemed OK – boring and predictable maybe – but OK. I'd never seen or heard them have any serious arguments. Geoff and Lucy got on well whenever we hung out with them. Of course that old saying of you never know what goes on behind closed doors is not just a saying, it's true, but I think we'd have picked up on any problems between Lucy and Geoff.

Which made me think. Had they picked up on our problems? Probably, yes. Did they really believe that I fell down the stairs that time Geoff took me to the hospital? Who knew. All this thinking got me absolutely nowhere. I wondered whether to mention this latest development – the gun acquisition – to our counsellor but decided against it. Chris would only kick off again. I'd had enough of that for a while.

Instead, I put it behind me and once again told myself that everything was fine. All the while ignoring the counsellor's voice in my head telling me that maybe I should start facing the realities in my life rather than air-brushing them out. Hmmph. What did she know? I was doing fine.

What we needed was a holiday. Hell, we hadn't been away properly since our Honeymoon. I thought I'd try to interest Chris in coming up with where we should go and booking it all. Another project for him. My life at the time revolved around trying to come up with things for him and us to do, to stop him thinking about alcohol. To try and show him that a good and happy life without alcohol was actually possible. I wasn't sure I was succeeding but I kidded myself I was. Did I mention I wasn't much good with reality?

I raised the subject while we were having dinner after one of our counselling sessions. I really wasn't sure if we were achieving anything from all this so-called therapy, and I kept on expecting Chris to call an end to it. But he seemed to get some kind of perverse enjoyment out of it all. I think what he liked was trying to get the better of the counsellor. He simply would not be drawn on questions about his childhood. She asked him why he was so reluctant to talk about it and he just said that there was nothing to say. End of. How do you deal with that? Well Jennifer (our therapist) dealt with it by frowning and making copious notes in her book, then clearing her throat and changing the subject. You could see though that she wasn't done with it yet. I wondered if she were going to suggest he took a polygraph at some stage. Or is that just something the police use? Or MI5 possibly? I think I was probably letting my imagination run wild; the use of a polygraph was unlikely to be in her arsenal of weapons. I wouldn't fancy taking one myself anyway…

Chris was always in a good mood after the sessions so it seemed an opportune time to raise the subject of a holiday.

"Remember I mentioned going on holiday?"

He looked up at me between mouthfuls of pasta but didn't say anything. I continued undaunted.

"What d'you think? It would be lovely to have a holiday together again, wouldn't it? We had a great time on our Honeymoon."

"Yeah, maybe."

Not a good start. God I could have done with some alcohol. Not only to fortify me but to accompany my wonderful meal. It was almost a crime to have authentic Italian food senza a glass of Pinot Grigio. But I'd promised not to drink in front of him, so that was that.

"Where d'you fancy going?" I was nothing if not persistent.

"Umm…" He trailed off as he shovelled more pasta into his mouth.

"You choose where we go, Chris. I picked Greece for our Honeymoon, so you choose. We could go somewhere in Europe again maybe? Somewhere not too far away?"

"Is that me choosing?"

"Oh no, sorry. Where do you want to go?"

"Not sure I do really."

"Why?" I was astonished. I reached for my non-existent

glass of wine and found a tumbler of iced water instead. Damn I needed a drink! Water just wasn't going to cut it.

"Do you remember the lovely meals we had on our Honeymoon Sarah?"

I nodded.

"And do you remember sharing a bottle or 2 of wine with them?"

I nodded again. I had a feeling I knew where this was going.

"Maybe you also remember our pre-dinner drinks we always had sitting outside somewhere whilst deciding where to go and eat?"

I looked down at my food and picked at the remnants with my fork.

"Of course. I remember it all. It was lovely."

"Well I remember it too. And I remember how enjoyable it all was. I also remember that I didn't once get drunk or nasty with you."

"Of course you didn't, but-"

"So my point is – I want to be able to do that again if we go on holiday. I mean have a drink. A holiday abroad without alcohol holds no interest for me. Being able to have a drink is all part of a holiday."

I picked up my glass of water and put it down again. Hadn't I just been gagging for some alcohol myself? OK I didn't have any, but I knew I could go home and sneak a whiskey while Chris was checking stuff on his computer, or whatever the hell it was he did on his computer every evening (actually, what the hell was it he did on his computer every evening?) Chris, on the other hand, could not have a drink. At all. Ever.

"But there are so many other things to a holiday Chris. There's being together! There's doing exciting things! New places to see, new experiences to be had! Sex! Do you remember the wonderful sex we had on our Honeymoon?"

"Made all the better by having a couple of drinks together beforehand."

Christ. He had me there. That was pretty much true. God, how to deal with this. Should I let him drink on holiday? Would it be OK? If he promises he will stop again? No, no no!! What are you thinking woman! He's an alcoholic for fuck's sake, he can't drink. Period.

"Right, well I don't really know what to say, Chris. Is this ever going to end? Are you ever going to forgive me for asking you to stop drinking?"

I pushed my plate away. He said nothing.

"How are you getting on at your AA meetings? Are they helping?"

"If you mean do they stop me from thinking about drink all the time then no, they're not helping. Apparently I'm a 'functional alcoholic', which is better than being a 'chronic' one but just as hard to deal with."

"Functional? I thought it was 'functioning'."

"So did I. It's not. Although 'high-functioning' is another term for it. But I'm actually neither at the moment am I, because I'm not drinking."

"But how are you able to do it? How are you able to just not drink? You make it look easy but I know it can't be."

"You're bloody right there, Sarah," He wiped his mouth on a napkin. "It's about as easy as it would be to get Phil to cut down on his lunch expenses. And you know how hard that is."

I smiled. He was making a joke. That was a good sign, surely.

"So how *do* you do it? How do you stop yourself picking up that drink?"

He looked into my eyes with his beautiful pools of blue.

"You, Sarah. I stop because I think of you."

Oh God. Tears welled up and I grabbed his hand.

"Chris, I'm so sorry for you. It must be awful. But it will get better – won't it? If you keep going to the meetings and we keep filling our lives with things, surely it will get better?"

"I hope so, Sarah. Because honestly, it's a living hell at times."

CHAPTER THIRTY-ONE

Meanwhile, back at the Agency, ad campaigns still carried on apace and with them, all thoughts of a holiday were most definitely on the long finger. Chris and I both threw ourselves into our work. At least we had that. Wonderful, all-consuming, fulfilling jobs to take our minds off things unpleasant.

Around this time, Phil ventured a question to me about Chris's drinking. We were working on, appropriately enough, a poster campaign for Gordon's Gin.

"How's Chris doing at the moment? Is he off the booze or something?"

I briefly wondered what the 'or something' meant, and then chose my words carefully.

"Yeah – he's giving it a break for a while. Just because, you know, because…" OK so I didn't choose my words *that* carefully. "Well, we should all give it a break every now and then, shouldn't we?"

Phil turned from his desk and looked at me. "Should we?" He seemed utterly confounded at the prospect.

"'Course we should. Give our body a rest and all that."

"So are you off it too?"

Whoops. "Err, not entirely."

He turned back to his sketching of a life-size Gordon's Gin bottle.

"So how long has he been off it then?"

Oh for fuck's sake. Phil rarely had conversations lasting more than two minutes with anyone, and here he was quizzing the life out of me.

"Umm – about three weeks or so I think. Why d'you ask?"

"Dunno really, just curious." He put his pencil down and scratched his increasingly-bald head. "Just that I've noticed him getting quite ratty in a couple of client meetings recently, and..."

"What's new there? Chris frequently gets ratty in client meetings."

"Yeah, but this was different. He just got up from the table, started pacing the room and then roared at the client for no apparent reason. Everyone was pretty shocked."

That got my full attention.

"Christ. What happened?"

"Well, he sat down, put his face in his hands briefly and apologised. Said he was really tired as he wasn't sleeping well."

"And you say that happened more than once?"

"Yeah, couple of times. Not exactly the same both times, but similar."

I put down the pen I realised I'd been chewing on for the last few minutes. What to say. Phil was clearly looking for something more from me. Should I confide in him? Wasn't Chris's alcoholism an open secret in the Agency anyway? Probably, yes, but I'd never admitted it or discussed it with anyone aside from Becky. Something to do with not facing reality (no surprises there)…or maybe just a streak of self-preservation.

Phil's silent back and slightly hunched shoulders spoke volumes. He knew there was more to this and, what's more, he knew that I knew that he knew.

"I s'pose it's fair to say that he's finding the not drinking hard to deal with. No great secret that Chris likes a drink, is it?"

Phil turned to look at me.

"I know this can't be easy for you, Sarah. Or for Chris of course, but I'm more concerned about you."

Oh God I was going to cry. I turned away quickly and picked up my pen again.

"Thanks, Phil. I think you know what we're dealing with here, but it's not something I'm comfortable discussing with anyone. It's bloody difficult, yes – but I don't want the whole Agency whispering about us and talking behind Chris's back."

A furtive glance at Phil's expression told me that that particular wish was too late. I changed tactics.

"Umm, can you help me here, Phil? Can you try and shut down the gossip?"

"I can try. But you know what this place is like." He got up and walked over to me. Shit, was he going to give me a hug?

"Look, try not to worry. Like every other bit of gossip, it will die down soon enough." He put his hand on my arm. Thank God he didn't go in for the full hug; I would have surely broken down if he had. "If there's anything I can do to help, Sarah, you will ask won't you?"

"I will, Phil. And thanks. Means a lot."

"OK, so where are we on this bloody campaign? Got any zinging words yet to go with my wonderful artwork?"

I smiled. Situation normal again, thank goodness.

CHAPTER THIRTY-TWO

Situation normal again, briefly, I should say. Phil and I were back to our usual working partnership, but other than that, things became anything but normal in a very short space of time.

Chris was still going to his AA meetings – or as I said, I assumed he was. He was definitely going somewhere every Wednesday evening after work. I didn't think he was drinking again – I certainly saw no signs of it. He didn't stay in town at all and he never went to the pub with the rest of the creative department when they decided they needed a drink. Which of course was fairly regularly. I didn't go that often either. Didn't think it was fair to Chris and also I didn't want to get cornered by some supposedly well-intentioned colleague asking with an almost-believable concerned face how Chris was. Simply wanting me to dish the dirt so that he or she could pass it on with glee.

I missed those sessions to be honest. But then I kept thinking that I could go to the pub any time I wanted. I could have a drink or two or three and know when to stop (mostly) and I would be fine. Chris, on the other hand, could not go to the pub. Well, technically he could, but he would either be putting himself at huge risk or be on the orange juice all night. Neither was appealing. I got that.

I was still mentoring the lovely student, James, although he had also started doing some work with other team members. I enjoyed his company and his creativity. We got on well and had a laugh together. I remember Chris catching sight of us coming back into the Agency after a dubbing session. We were giggling about something – quite uncontrollably I seem to recall. The sort of giggling I normally only display after several vodkas and tonic, but something – I forget what – had really tickled my fancy. I'll never forget the look on Chris's face. Pure anger. I smiled at him and went over to start telling him about whatever it was we were laughing at, but he turned away with the words 'Gotta go.' James didn't seem to notice (he was still giggling) but it brought me back to my senses pretty quick. Shit. But then I thought – for fuck's sake – can't I have a laugh with another man? Because that's all it was. A bit of fun.

It came as no surprise to me whatsoever that Chris decided to bring the subject up when we were both at home that evening.

"You seemed to be enjoying yourself with that toy boy of yours today."

Even though I was expecting it, it still floored me momentarily. Damn it, Chris had a way of doing that!

"Don't be silly, we were just having a laugh."

"Looked like more than that to me. You were both giggling ridiculously. Almost hanging on to each other."

"That is NOT true!" I was hugely indignant at the accusation. "We weren't touching each other at all, just bloody laughing. Is that a crime Chris? To have a laugh with another man?"

I briefly wondered if I'd gone too far. If he'd been drinking, this interaction would certainly have ended somewhat differently. But as far as I could tell, he was perfectly sober. Miffed and talking crap, but sober.

"When did you and I last laugh like that Sarah?"

Ummm…

"Dunno, Chris. We don't seem to laugh much these days do we?"

"No. And do you know why? Because life is sodding boring, that's why."

Right. Here we go again.

"Is there nothing in this whole wide world that would make you happy, apart from being able to drink again?"

He turned to stare out of the window.

"I don't know. I'm trying, really I am, but it doesn't seem to be getting any easier."

"But it's still early days. You're going to the meetings right? And we're having counselling. I know we have a way to go yet, but we'll get there."

I walked over to him and put my arms around him.

"I love you Chris. We'll get through this."

He nuzzled my neck.

"I was so jealous seeing you having a good time with James. My first thought was that you'd been out drinking together."

"You don't need a drink to have a laugh. You just have to find something funny."

He looked at me then, his mouth twitching. "You don't say darling."

We both smiled at this, then hugged and kissed. Another hurdle hurdled.

Remember what I said about the 'brief situation normal' thing? Well this wasn't what caused the upsetting of the apple cart. Oh no. That was something way bigger.

Chapter Thirty-three

Not long after this incident, Chris had another tantrum during a client meeting. It was pretty bad, from what I heard. This time the client didn't accept Chris's apology and instead marched straight out of the meeting and into the Managing Director's office. I was told all of this by a gleeful colleague. I was going to say friend, but that would be disrespectful to my friends.

The upshot of it was that our dear, sweet MD – Alistair – called Chris into his office for a chat. I'll never know exactly what was said but it resulted in Chris being given three weeks temporary leave at home to 'sort himself out'. That bit was verbatim. Full pay, mind you, so not too bad. Well, not too bad if you weren't a recovering alcoholic.

When Chris told me the news that night, my first thought was Oh God; he's going to start drinking again for sure. How can he NOT start drinking?

I let him talk without interrupting. Wishing all the time that I had a glass of wine in front of me from which to seek some comfort. He said that he'd just lost his patience in the meeting and couldn't control his temper. He then told me about the previous two times, which I reacted to with raised eyebrows, signifying (I hoped) surprise. When he finished his tale, we remained silent for a while.

Eventually I plucked up the courage to speak.

"Why do you think you reacted that way, Chris?"

"Oh for God's sake, Sarah, you sound like our fucking Counsellor! I don't know." He started pacing the kitchen floor. "I think it's because I don't care anymore. I simply don't care if I upset a client, or even if we lose the business. I have no patience with them. They're all morons."

Right. Tough one.

"But it's our job, Chris. You've been cross with clients before, but it was always because you were passionate about the creative work, because you firmly believed in what you were presenting. These last few incidents, from what you've said, are different."

"Yes. Like I said, I just don't care."

"But why?"

He looked at me.

"Do you really need to ask? Isn't it bloody obvious? My life has changed. I don't care about anything anymore."

"But you said…"

"I still care about you, Sarah, if that's what you were going to say."

"It wasn't, but good to know." I swept a few crumbs off the kitchen counter. "It's not enough though is it?"

"What's not?"

"Caring about me. It's not enough to make you happy is it? Or to give you any kind of fulfilling life?"

He leaned against the kitchen sink and hung his head.

"I don't know what to say. I think maybe you'd be better off without me."

"No way, Chris." I went to him and put my hands on his shoulders. "Look at me." He slowly lifted his head so that I could stare into his pools of blue. "We're in this together. I'm not giving up on you. OK? We'll do it. We'll do it together." He put his head on my shoulder and cried like a baby.

Oh God. Never mind whether Chris had any faith in me or not, I wasn't sure *I* even believed my own words. How can alcohol play such a big part in someone's life? To the extent that their life is almost not worth living without it? How did it have such a hold? If only he could have a couple of drinks now and then – something to look forward to at the weekend maybe. Could he do that? I very nearly suggested it but everything I'd read about alcoholism was screaming 'No!' at me.

"Chris, you've got to start looking at the positives in your life. The things you enjoy. There is so much more to life than alcohol. I know it's easy for me to say that, but really, if you think about it, there are loads of things that give you pleasure in life, aren't there?"

He sniffed and grunted without looking at me. I took this as an encouraging sign and continued.

"You've got some work to do at home haven't you? Some campaigns to work on? Put your heart and soul into them! Make them the best bloody campaigns ever! Remind the Agency why you're our Creative Director, and a bloody good one too. Go for a cycle, go for a run, go shooting if you must, hang out with me and watch silly programmes on TV. Let's go to the cinema! When did we last do that? And we've still got our lovely counselling sessions to look forward to …"

He slowly lifted his head and looked at me.

"You were doing quite well up till that point missus. Blown it now"

I smiled. Bit of the old Chris coming back again thank goodness.

"You love our counselling sessions! You absolutely love trying to get the better of her, don't you? Come on, admit it!"

"OK yes, I do. They think they're some damned clever, these people, but you can see right through them and their sodding unending questions. I do treat it as a bit of a game, yeah."

"So will you try and give life your best shot for a while? I will help you all I can, Chris, I promise."

"What can I say? I have the best wife. I will, as you say, give it my best shot."

An unfortunate choice of words on my part as it turned out.

CHAPTER THIRTY-FOUR

What I wouldn't give to work from home for a couple of weeks! No setting the alarm at some ungodly hour, no jostling with the other poor sods on the underground and no fucking 'knowing' looks from work colleagues. 'Cos that's what I got the whole time Chris was away from the office. It nearly drove me mad. Oh I rode it out OK – just stared at some of them as if to say 'You got a problem mate? Come on then, say it!' None of them ever did of course. It was just the looks. And the conversations that would stop whenever I approached certain groups of people. I had my few loyal friends there of course, who did their best to support me, and I also had Phil who protected me endlessly. In the end I just got used to it and shrugged it off. Obviously not much going on in their own lives if they had to take such an active interest in mine. So there.

Chris, of course, was not in the know about any of this. I don't think he'd ever been aware of the gossip or the looks to be honest, which was a good thing. Surprisingly, he did OK at home. At least, on the face of it he did. He appeared to be working hard on the jobs with which he'd been allowed to continue, and he had several phone conversations with me, plus other members of the creative department. He was going out every day on his bike or for a run, which was great. He travelled up to London for his weekly AA meeting and continued to have daily phone calls from his sponsor. Could this be the making of him I dared wonder? Probably not, a voice in my head quickly countered.

Every time I came home from work I had a jolly good but extremely surreptitious search of the house for evidence of any drinking. I never found any. So either he wasn't drinking or he was very good at concealing it. He never appeared to have had a drink, that was for sure. I briefly toyed with the idea of asking him how he was managing to resist the booze, but decided that would be tantamount to begging for an argument. I just took each day at a time and breathed a sigh of relief every night when I climbed into bed. He seemed OK to me, but the absence of any joy from his life was still palpable.

I racked my brains to think of something novel for us to do during his three week 'punishment'; anything that might restore some sort of normality to our lives. I came up with the exciting idea of going to see his Mum and also of paying my parents a visit. What's not to like about that? Both suggestions were met with what you might call a somewhat muted response.

"We haven't seen your Mum or my parents for ages Chris – little daytrip together might be nice?" I filled the ensuing silence with a fierce chopping of carrots. "I mean, they'd like it for sure and we really should see more of them." I murdered a few more carrots. "Shouldn't we?" At this point I turned towards him, forcing him to answer me.

"S'pose so, yeah."

"I can understand the reluctance to see my parents, but your Mum? Why wouldn't you want to see her? She's all on her own and her only other child is miles away across the Atlantic."

"I know, Sarah, I do know that, thank you. And if you cast your mind back to just a few seconds ago, I agreed to your plan."

I resumed my dinner preparations.

"You sort of agreed, yes, but you don't seem that enthralled with the idea. Like I said, visiting my parents is a bit of a chore for you – I get that – but what is it with seeing your Mum?"

"For Christ's sake Sarah, give up on the sodding Spanish Inquisition will you! I said I'd do it – both of the visits – so just leave it at that!" He stormed out of the kitchen and thundered up the stairs.

Call me sensitive but something told me I'd touched a nerve. A hitherto unknown one really. We didn't see a lot of his Mum but he phoned her regularly and they appeared to me to have a good relationship. The lack of any mention of his father between the two of them was still a mystery to me, but I had given up trying to solve that particular conundrum ages ago. Why on earth didn't he want to see his Mum?

Well see his Mum we did. That weekend we went up for the day on Saturday. It was about an hour's drive. We didn't say much to each other throughout the journey. Chris didn't ask me anything about work and I decided to avoid the subject also. We kept the chat light and uncontentious.

His Mum was overjoyed to see us. She had lunch ready and made such a fuss. Well mainly of Chris – or should I say Chrissy...I had to smother a snigger every time she called him that. Chris was brilliant, I have to say. The model son. Answered his mother's multitude of questions about everything, without of course mentioning his enforced stay at home, and asked her about her cat and her garden. I loved seeing him like this. He was animated, lovely, loving and, well, just gorgeous. We went for a walk around his Mum's village after lunch and then, as if we hadn't had enough to eat to sustain us for a couple of weeks already, tea and a homemade cake were produced.

You might think by now that this was all going swimmingly and be convinced that it could end no other way but well. I'm afraid you'd be wrong. I thought the same and I myself was wrong. Very wrong. I was sitting there, tucking into my slice of delicious, if slightly over-marged, Victoria Sponge thinking, 'well this is good. So pleased we did this. We must do it more often.' And then…boom!

Chris's Mum offered him a drink.

"Will you have a glass of whiskey before you go, Chrissy? I've got your favourite in the cupboard. Been keeping it for when you next came…"

"No, Mum, I won't thanks."

"Aww Chrissy – why not? You love whiskey! And your favourite! I'll even keep you company with a small sherry!"

"No thanks, Mum."

If only she had let it lie there.

"Have you gone off whiskey, darling? Would you like something else?"

"I said no thanks, Mum. I'm driving."

"But can't Sarah drive? You can drive dear can't you?" She turned towards me.

I nodded my head mutely.

"For Christ's sake Mum I said NO! How many more times? Will you PLEASE stop asking me! I don't want a drink!"

My goodness, the silence that followed. I didn't know where to look. His poor Mum was distraught. She was trying to fight off tears. Clearly he'd never shouted at her like that before. I felt so sorry for her but didn't know how best to react. I didn't want to anger Chris further by comforting her.

After a few minutes, Chris shook his head and sighed.

"I'm sorry, Mum. I shouldn't have shouted at you." And to my eternal joy, he went over and gave her a kiss. "I'm sorry, OK? Are you all right?"

She sniffed and nodded. "'Course I am. Silly me for going on and on. Will you have another cup of tea?"

The drive home was an interesting one. Silence for the first few miles whilst I summoned up the courage to say something.

"What just happened there?"

"Hmm? What d'you mean?

OK, we'll play it that way if you want.

"I mean with your Mum. Why did she keep pushing for you to have a drink?" I thought it best to make her out to be the bad guy here. Initially anyway.

"She always does that. Haven't you noticed before? Probably not I s'pose, because I used to have a drink generally whenever we visited her. You remember that? You usually drove home."

"Yes, I guess."

"I knew what happened was going to happen. That's why I didn't want to visit her."

"But if you knew it was going to happen, you could have prevented it from happening."

"What, by having a drink? You're kidding aren't you?"

"No, not by having a drink – I meant by not getting worked up about it and shouting at her."

He thought about that for a while.

"Yeah, I could have done, but I didn't, did I? Not that nice a person I guess."

"You're a lovely person, Chris! You were so lovely to her all day and you made it up to her when you realised how upset she was. I just don't get why it irked you so much."

"Why does anything irk me these days? Look at work. Look at the arguments you and I have sometimes. It's the constant stress of having to stay off the booze for Christ's sake."

Right. So my wonderful plan had backfired yet again. I was running out of ideas for saving our marriage. Maybe it was simply beyond salvation. Either way, I didn't hold out much hope that the planned trip to my parents next weekend was going to pull it back from the brink.

Chapter Thirty-five

The following Sunday morning, all was well. At least on the face of it. We were about to embark on a visit to my parents, so that put a bit of dampener on the beautiful sunny day to which we awoke. With hindsight, I was probably always a little hard on my parents. They were a bit odd – stuck in their ways I suppose – but they had my best interests at heart. Mostly. I think Mum going on about me having a baby was probably more in her interest than mine. Dad was always fairly laid back and non-judgemental, which I should have appreciated more in those early days. I suppose they just seemed a bit boring to me, but I guess most parents do when you yourself are in your twenties and having the time of your life.

Anyway, I always quite enjoyed seeing them but was generally equally pleased when it was time to leave. I knew that Chris never really 'got' them and that they annoyed him a bit, although he did have quite a good relationship with my Dad. I often wondered what his relationship had been like with *his* Dad…but of course that whole subject was off limits.

On the journey there, I spent some time trying to come up with a reason why Chris wasn't drinking. I was hoping to avoid a rerun of the incident at his Mum's place.

"Shall I tell Mum and Dad that you're on antibiotics?"

"Umm, why would you do that?"

"So that they don't keep offering you a drink like your Mum did."

He thought about that for a while.

"Yeah, whatever." Was the best he could come up with.

"I'm just trying to avoid another situation like last weekend. Don't you think it's a good idea?"

"Your parents aren't like my Mum; they won't keep asking."

"But they might. And you might get cross again."

"I won't, Sarah. But do what you want, tell them that if you want. I don't care."

There it was again. Apathy…disinterest…call it what you will, but he was displaying it more and more these days.

I sighed. God this never got any easier.

My first thought on seeing my parents was that they looked older. I immediately felt guilty and made a silent promise that I would make an effort to visit them more frequently. With or without Chris. They were very pleased to see us of course. I was ushered inside like the prodigal daughter. Drinks were offered and I decided to get way ahead of the game by saying straight out that Chris wasn't drinking because he was on antibiotics. Mum gave me one of those 'Knowing Mother' looks but immediately sympathised with Chris, saying she hoped he was OK. She then asked what the antibiotics were for; something I had failed to anticipate. Chris looked at me for guidance – or was it just a totally pissed-off look? I wasn't sure – but after a moment's hesitation I said, "oh he's had a bit of a throat infection but it's nearly gone now. Just got to finish the old medication, you know how it is."

Phew. Got away with that. Just.

We migrated to the lounge and sat down. And then, just like Chris's Mum, my Mother started interrogating me. Clearly a mother's prerogative.

"How's work, dear? What are you working on at the moment?"

I started to tell her about my latest campaign, but I could see her eyes glazing over. Mum didn't really understand what I did. I think she just thought I sat around penning a few words here and there and going to the pub a lot. Not a bad summation of my job I suppose. Dad showed more interest though and asked a few pertinent questions. He also included Chris in the conversation which worried me as I thought he might inadvertently alert them to the fact that he'd been working at home. He did. They didn't comment though – perhaps assumed it was a 'creative' thing to do every now and then. Mum jumped back in again.

"Still enjoying your work and all that commuting, Sarah?"

"I love my job, Mum. Commuting's a bit of a bind yeah, but you get used to it."

"Takes up so much of your day, dear, doesn't it? Must be very tiring. You don't get to spend much time in that lovely house of yours."

I knew exactly where this was leading and tried to head her off at the pass.

"We're very happy with our lives at the moment. We're lucky that we both enjoy our jobs and we have the weekends then to enjoy our home. It's good Mum, really."

I failed to head her off at the pass.

"Oh. No chance of a grandchild yet then, I s'pose?"

"Ellen, for goodness' sake!" Good old Dad to the rescue. "You shouldn't ask questions like that."

Mum looked suitably admonished but wasn't done with it yet.

"Well I know, but you can't leave these things too late can you, and Sarah will be 30 next year!"

"Mum – women are having children later in life these days. Mid-thirties ... older even. It's our choice and I promise you'll be the first to know if and when it happens but please don't keep asking me about it." I threw Chris a look and noticed that he was shifting uncomfortably in his seat. He reached for his glass of water, clearly wishing it would miraculously turn into wine.

Fortunately Mum dropped the subject. Later in the day, however, she touched on another raw nerve. Were we having a holiday this year? Wasn't it ages since our last holiday together? In fact, had we even been away since our Honeymoon? I swear she had a checklist of things to bring up every time she saw me, most of them seemingly designed to make my life even more difficult than it already was. I managed to deflect the holiday questions by saying we were in the process of thinking about our next trip and no, we hadn't decided where yet. Thank God I was able to have a drink; it certainly helped me navigate the troubled waters of eternal questions around Chris's and my life together.

We managed to escape in the early evening, shortly after a monologue from Mum about my sister Caroline. Seems she was an even greater disappointment to our Mother than I was. I took some small comfort in that, whilst simultaneously feeling guilty about it. Poor Caroline – she'd really made a balls of her life so far. Unlike me of course. I was doing just great...

Usual silence at first on the drive home whilst we both

independently digested how the visit had gone. I was still resolved to see more of my parents, even though Mum had managed to irritate me.

"I'm sorry about Mum always going on about having babies. It's a pain, isn't it?"

"Somewhat, yep."

"She means well."

"Does she?"

"Yes…sort of anyway. And, actually, you and I did have a conversation a while back about starting a family."

"And your point is?"

"My point is that we have thought about it, haven't we?"

"No, you thought about it, I didn't. I don't want a child."

"What – ever?"

"Maybe, but certainly not at the moment. Don't you think I have enough on my plate as it is?"

I didn't respond to that. I was reeling. Children had always been a part of my plan. Oh I know I always put Mum off whenever she brought the subject up, but that was because it was none of her business and because I really didn't want a baby just yet. But I sure as hell did at some point in my life. Chris did too – we had discussed it, hadn't we? Maybe we hadn't properly, maybe I just assumed…

"That's potentially a big problem, Chris," I turned to look at him. "I definitely want kids at some stage. I thought you did too."

"I did yes, not sure I do any more though."

Was he *punishing* me? Was this some kind of revenge on his part because I'd made him give up the drink? Surely he wouldn't steep that low.

"Do you mean that?" I tried but failed to discern his

expression. "Actually, it's probably not a good time to talk about this. I mean while you're still coming to terms with not drinking and all that. I'm sorry I brought it up."

"Coming to terms with not drinking? How simple you make it sound, darling. But then of course you don't have to do it, do you? You don't have to 'come to terms with not drinking'. Enjoy your couple of glasses of wine today, did you? I could see very well that you did. Every last fucking drop. Thought you'd promised not to drink in front of me? That didn't last long did it? How do you think I felt? God what I wouldn't have given to have had a drink with you all. It was bloody torture, Sarah – you know that? Fucking torture!"

Well that ended well. Much like the previous weekend's outing. Nice one Sarah, great suggestions, both of them. Where the hell do I go from here?

Chapter Thirty-six

Drinking with Becky of course. That was my first thought and that's exactly what I did. Not immediately you understand, but the event was planned that very evening. Probably not the kindest thing to do to Chris, given the circumstances, but I was sick of pandering to him and trying to come up with solutions to what was essentially his problem. Well, no, it was very much my problem too. But either way, I was sick of it. Hell, I needed a bit of fun and that was always guaranteed whenever Becks and I got together for a few drinks.

Wednesday evening after work was to be the big night. Normally when I went out drinking with Becky during the week I had every intention of catching the last train home. I often didn't of course, but the intention was always there. This time however, I elected to cut out the middleman and decided upfront NOT to catch the last train home. I would stay with Becky and go into work the next day from her place.

I did feel a bit guilty when I informed Chris of my plan, saying I'd see him on Thursday evening after work. He was still at home – his last week – and I guess, looking back, it was a bit cruel of me. But I was so fed up. My plans of trying to restore some normality in our lives had backfired spectacularly; we were getting on worse than ever. He still seemed to be coping OK with being at home but, if I were honest, I didn't really know *how* he was coping because we barely spoke. I knew I had to get away and also I knew I needed a good chat with Becky about the situation. I expected some narky, sarcastic comments from him when I delivered the news, but he just grunted. That was probably worse actually. I didn't know how to deal with that kind of reaction.

My night with Becks certainly lived up to expectations. We hit one of our favourite wine bars in Oxford Street and were soon deep in conversation and even deeper in Pinot Grigio.

"So how's it going with Chris working at home?"

"Umm, bit up and down I s'pose. It was OK at first – he really seemed to be handling it well – but it's gone to shit the last few days."

"How so?"

I told her about the disastrous visits to our respective parents.

"Weird about his Mum and the drink isn't it?" Becky knocked back some more of her wine. "What do you think that was about?"

"Dunno. There's definitely something fishy in that family around alcohol." I topped up our glasses. "And I don't mean the obvious with Chris being an alcoholic. They all have a strange relationship with it. I told you about the references Jane has made to his drinking and things from the past?"

"Yes, but you never got to the bottom of those things, did you?"

"No. I never pushed her or asked her anything much. Maybe I should have."

"Not too late. Perhaps now's a good time?"

159

I nodded pensively. Becks had hit the nail on the head as usual. I didn't pursue any of the hints Jane had given me because, typically, I had my head in the sand and didn't want to know.

"I just don't make him happy anymore, Becky. Well, I do occasionally, but there's a sadness about him. You know – an emptiness? He can't seem to enjoy life fully without alcohol. I don't think he's ever going to change."

"Christ, Sarah, that's a tough one. What the fuck to do?" She signalled to one of the waiters to bring us over another bottle. "I don't know what to say. Shit situation."

"But do I keep trying or do I just give up on him?"

"Well, I think you know what I feel about that, but you still love him, don't you?"

"Yup. That's the sodding problem. I do. I don't know why – there's not much of the old Chris left to love anymore." The waiter brought our wine over and we both took a moment to admire his physique as he expertly pulled the cork from the bottle.

"Ladies? May I top you up?" His wicked smile was delicious.

"Oh any time!" We chorused and then collapsed into helpless giggles. Our man, clearly used to dealing with slightly pissed young women, simply grinned as he refilled our glasses.

"Just give me a shout if there's anything you need." And with a wink and another wicked smile, he was gone.

"Bloody hell! He's gorgeous, isn't he? Where did they find him? He was definitely looking at you more than me Sarah. You're in there!" Becky was always in denial about her attraction to the opposite sex. "I'll fight you for him though!"

We laughed again. "You're on!" I challenged.

"Seriously though, do you think I should stop drinking to help Chris with his problem?"

"God no! He's the one with the problem, not you. Although I say that…"

"Yeah, yeah, I know I like my drink as well, but I *can* live without it and I do know when to stop…mostly. Chris, on the other hand can't and doesn't. What am I saying, he's clearly an alcoholic and I'm not."

"Yup – quite."

"But I was thinking that it would be a nice thing to do, to support him. If I could do it…I could try for a while couldn't I? I don't drink in front of him a lot at all, but I did at my parents and that really got to him."

"Do it if you want, Sarah, but I don't think that's going to solve anything here."

"So what *do* I do then?"

"You finish that glass of wine and then have another one and we will now change the subject. Because you know what I think, but in the end it's your decision. I've told you I'll always be there for you no matter what – you know that, right?"

OK Becks, fair enough. We were always talking about my situation. She was very good and loyal but it must have been boring sometimes.

I did as she said. An hour or so later, we ordered a third bottle of wine. That was a mistake. Half way through it we started serenading each other with half-remembered songs from various musicals. We thought it was hilarious and very entertaining, but apparently most of the other customers didn't. And the staff certainly didn't. Our lovely waiter was still smiling but he was quite firm in telling us that we had to leave the premises. Now. We didn't argue – just blew him a kiss, grabbed our jackets and made it outside before collapsing on top of each other in a giggling heap.

Shame. I always liked that wine bar. But it would be some time before I showed my face there again.

Chapter Thirty-seven

We managed to find a taxi willing to drive us to Becky's flat, where it took us a good ten minutes to get the key in the lock, due to a lot of giggling and sliding down the wall. Somehow, again, Ed was alerted to our arrival home. What a hero that man was! He just helped us inside, gave us both a pint glass of water to down and pointed me in the direction of the already made up couch. Such a sweetheart.

"You're so lucky, Becky. I want Ed. Can I have Ed, please? Just for a loan? He's *soooooo* sweet." At which point, much to Ed's horror, I started stroking his face.

Becky, of course, just burst out laughing. "Have him! He's yours! Just on loan as you say, mind. I will need him back!"

How we laughed! Ed, being stone cold sober, didn't.

"No seriously Becks, you are lucky. I'm married to a fucking arsehole drunk and you have lovely Ed to come home to. I want an Ed."

Many a true word spoken in drink they say, or something like that.

Ed decided this was getting into dodgy territory and so herded Becky towards their bedroom. "Night Sarah – sleep well."

"Night lovely Ed! Night night Becky – love you!"

"Love you too, Sez. Great night wasn't it? Until we got thrown out of the wine bar!" Cue more laughing and a final bedroom-facing shove from Ed.

I didn't think I'd be able to sleep at all but I went out like a light. It's possible that the wine had something to do with that. Amazingly enough – probably thanks to Ed's foresight with the pint of water – I felt OK enough to go to work the next day. Although clearly I didn't look as OK as I felt.

"Christ, Sarah – what happened to you? You look like you pulled an all-nighter. Or maybe you're just getting old?"

"Cheers, Phil! Bloody good night out with Becky. Just what I needed to be honest. Hilarious – we got thrown out of Pastels! Actually, that doesn't seem quite so funny now. Bit embarrassing, to be honest. Ah well, we live and learn don't we?"

Phil smiled at me. "Do we, Sarah? I don't know. If you say so. How're things at home?"

I dumped my bag under the desk and sat down heavily.

"Umm, not sure how to answer that." I started fiddling with a pen top. "He seems to be staying off the drink – well he *is* staying off the drink – but he's not happy. At all. It's pretty shit actually."

"Well maybe he'll be happier when he comes back to work next week. D'you think? Is he ready?"

I wondered briefly whether Phil had his own self interests at heart when enquiring about Chris's well-being. After all, Phil had been given the opportunity to take on more creative responsibility with Chris away. He had, in effect, been acting as the Agency's Creative Director in Chris's absence. I'd tried not to think how Chris might react to that – he surely knew that someone had to step into the breach, but he'd always had a thing about Phil coveting his job. I never saw it as a problem. I didn't think for one minute that Phil was Creative Director material.

"Yeah, probably. Everyone will be looking at him and talking about him of course, but he doesn't seem to notice that, does he? I hope he'll be OK. He'll need our support, Phil." I hoped I'd made my point, without actually making any point at all.

I'd called Chris on my way to work and he'd sounded fine. Asked if I'd had a good time and if I felt OK. I played down the amount of drink we'd had and didn't tell him about being thrown out of the wine bar. That made me sad. I shouldn't have to keep that from my husband. Look at the way Ed had treated us. Didn't give a shit that we were pissed or that we woke him up. Isn't that a more normal way for a partner to behave? To support you, to allow you your fun, to be there for you? I suddenly felt hard done by and angry with Chris. Not for the first time it crossed my mind that we were finished. That we'd be better off apart. But surely that would send him back to the drink? Was that my fault? Was that my responsibility? Oh God I didn't know. I was just going around in circles in my head and getting nowhere, as per usual.

Chapter Thirty-eight

I delayed my departure from the Agency that evening. I was working on a particularly complex brief but I wondered if, subconsciously, I really didn't want to go home and face the music. Or 'Chris', as I generally called him. Oh he'd been fine on the phone but I just knew he was going to give me a hard time about my night out.

Half of me still felt guilty about it – not about getting drunk and being thrown out of a wine bar, that was par for the course (although it was a first in terms of a wine bar ban) – but for going out and drinking and having a good time when I knew Chris was not able to do the same. The other half of me was saying 'for God's sake girl, you deserved a night out. You are trying your best to help him with his problem but he's not making it easy.' No wonder I couldn't conjure up any acceptable copy for my Trebor Softmints poster ad with an argument raging inside my head. Eventually I gave up on trying to encapsulate in one line why Trebor made softer and mintier mints than any other company, and headed out the door to the Tube. I hoped against hope that my train home would be delayed.

It wasn't. For once it was bang on time. I arrived home not much later than I normally would.

"Hi Chris! I'm home!" I decided to kick things off in a jovial manner. Nothing like a bit of optimism.

I was surprised to find him in the kitchen, preparing our dinner. I shouldn't have been surprised because that's what he'd done every weeknight for the last three weeks. But normally he waited for me and we cooked together.

"Mmm smells lovely – what is it?"

"Chicken chasseur. Nothing special." He didn't turn around to look at me or greet me in any way.

"Can I do something? You started without me! Nice treat! I'm a bit wrecked."

Shit. Red rag to a bull.

"Course you are, you had a late night didn't you?"

"Err, yes, spose it was quite late. We had a good old chat, Becky and I, it was really good to see her." I tried to deflect the inevitable sarcasm and nasty comments that were undoubtedly coming my way any second now.

"Have a good few drinks?" He still hadn't turned around to look at me or engage with me in any way.

"We had a few, yes." Because I can do that Chris, I can drink a lot one night and then not have anything for a couple of nights, because I'm not a RAGING ALCOHOLIC.

"Good. So happy for you." He banged the plates down on the sideboard and started dishing out the casserole.

I didn't know whether to ignore or point out his childish behaviour. Either could provoke an unwanted argument. I settled for the former and tried changing the subject;

"You know that brief for the Trebor Softmints poster? I'm finding it quite tough. Could you help me with it?"

Which ended up provoking an entirely different argument.

167

"What Trebor Softmints brief? I didn't see one." He put the plates on the table and we both sat down.

Shit, shit, shit! It had come directly from Phil, now I thought about it. Chris hadn't even been consulted on it. Talk about putting your foot right in it.

"Oh umm, well it must have come in while you were working at home."

"Right. But I'm still the fucking Creative Director; it should have come through me. Which fucking suit is responsible for that? That twat Oliver? The one who's still wet behind the ears? My God he's going to get it on Monday."

Losing his temper with one of the junior 'suits' was the very last thing Chris should do immediately upon returning to work after an enforced stay at home for losing his temper. I wondered if he would see the irony. Doubt it.

"Probably not his fault Chris – I'd say it just go overlooked. Have they been keeping you in the loop on everything else while you've been at home?"

"God knows Sarah. Your guess is as good as mine. They damn well should have been, yes. Unless someone else was doing my job for me."

I swallowed my mouthful as quickly as I could. "This is really good, Chris – thank you. Have you made it before? I don't remember. Where did you get the recipe?"

As usual – and God knows why I never learned this – my prattling had zero impact on deterring his line of thought.

"Have they, Sarah?"

"Have they what?"

"Been doing my job for me?" He put down his fork and focused his beautiful blue eyes on me.

"I wouldn't call it doing your job." I averted his gaze.

"What would you call it then? And who's been doing it?"

"Well Phil's been taking the odd brief from the senior suits but…I honestly thought you were included in them too." I didn't. I lied. I knew he wasn't included and it worried me hugely at the time but I couldn't get involved.

I was expecting an explosion, but he surprised me.

"Well that will all change on Monday." He picked up his fork again and resumed eating. "Phil will have to be reminded of exactly who the boss is. And it ain't him. They're not going to get rid of me that easily."

"What d'you mean? They don't want to get rid of you! I've told you before; Phil would not make a good Creative Director. Any fool can see that. Just come back and do your job. You're brilliant at it. You just have to be careful, that's all."

"Of what?" He wiped his mouth

"Of your temper of course! Of what got you your three week stay at home. You can't behave like that again, Chris. You know that, don't you?"

He got up and went towards the sink, pausing with his back to me.

"I do know that, yes. But thank you for pointing out the bleedin' obvious."

I went over and put my arms around him.

"Chris, Chris this is so hard for you, I know. But you're doing great. You've had three weeks at home on your own and you haven't touched the drink! That's amazing! I'm so proud of you. You can do this, I know you can."

He put his chin on top of my head and pulled me close.

"I'm trying Sarah, God knows I'm trying. For you. For us. I want to be happy again, I really do."

My heart broke for him at that point. My sweet, gorgeous

169

Chris. I loved him, without a doubt I loved him. I could never leave him.

"I know! Let's go to the cinema tomorrow evening. I'll leave work early and we'll have a nice evening out. Maybe go to the pizza place too? Give you a break from the cooking."

"And what's wrong with my cooking?" He pulled back to look me in the eyes.

"Oh absolutely nothing! It's lovely! I just meant-"

"I know what you meant, it's OK. I'm only teasing."

And there he was again, my beautiful Chris. We hugged and kissed and all was well with the world. Momentarily.

CHAPTER THIRTY-NINE

Actually, we had a great weekend. Went to the cinema Friday evening and the pizza place after. We laughed a lot, we chatted a lot; it was just like old times. Old times without the alcohol.

On Saturday we went for a long cycle together, stopping at a café en route for coffee and homemade scones. I was trying my best to show Chris that he could have a good time without drinking. Excellent coffee and delicious homemade scones beat alcohol in my book. Well at 2:00 p.m. on a Saturday afternoon they did anyway; 8:00 p.m. on a Saturday evening – or any given evening really – might be a different story, granted.

On Sunday Chris went shooting with Geoff and the gang, something I still hated but had come to accept. We had an agreement that we didn't discuss it at all on his return. As soon as I saw him heading for the cabinet where he kept his rifle, I disappeared rabbit-like upstairs so that I didn't have to look at him handling the loathsome thing. It was barbaric in my book. I couldn't understand how anyone could shoot an innocent, sweet animal or bird just for the hell of it. But I'd had to let it go. It was one of the few things that Chris sustained an interest in, and it meant time spent with other people who weren't work colleagues. It was good for him in that sense. He always returned home in a pleasant mood. I knew that they all went to the pub afterwards and I couldn't for the life of me work out how Chris managed that. It must have been torture for him. He always drove and picked up Geoff so maybe that was his get-out; the fact that he was driving. Still, it must have been tough going. Also Geoff surely would have offered to drive sometimes? Geoff had to be in the know, I concluded.

All too quickly, Monday morning came around and with it a lot of apprehension on my part. How were they going to treat him in work? How was he going to fare? Was he going to give someone a bollocking about leaving him out of the loop? Was he going to punish Phil by not signing his lunch expenses?

If Chris himself had any misgivings about returning to work, he did a good job of masking them. Was even pretty jovial I'd say, as we made our way to the train station. I toyed with the idea of reminding him to be on his best behaviour at the agency, but reasoned that that was the sort of thing you might say to a child, rather than to one's fully grown husband.

I did my level best to ignore the inevitable furtive looks and the odd smirk from co-workers as we walked through the creative department. One or two people who passed us even ventured something along the lines of 'Hi Chris! Great to see you back! We missed you!' I searched for the hidden meaning or the whiff of sarcasm, but to be honest I couldn't locate either of them. Chris deserved a bleedin' Oscar! He smiled at everyone he encountered and greeted them like long-lost friends. Made jokes about his 'holiday' and referred to them being the poor suckers fighting their way to work every morning on public transport while he was languishing at home. Oh how they all laughed!

But every one of them knew exactly why Chris had been languishing at home for three weeks, and I'd wager that every one of them also knew about his drinking problem. Possibly not the extent of it, but certainly the existence of it.

The first couple of days went well. Chris was catching up on everything, calling into his staff's offices to chat to them and to see what they were working on. I was interested to see how he was going to handle Phil when he came to see us, but he was perfectly friendly with him. Phil was a little aloof, I felt. I was never sure exactly what he thought of Chris. I knew he was after his job and I also knew that he was fond of me so maybe he felt a little protective? I don't know. Again, Chris either didn't notice his aloofness or he was still putting on a great act.

Alistair, our delightful MD, had been away for a couple of days so it wasn't until the Wednesday that Chris was called into his office. I only found out he was in there when the creative secretary stuck her head 'round our door barking:

"Phil – Alistair wants to see you. In his office. Now. Chris is there too."

Phil shot me a glance but said nothing. His guess was as good as mine. What the hell? All hope of any creativity for the next while was lost. Instead I grabbed a coffee and even hit the vending machine for a bar of chocolate which I almost NEVER did, before returning to my office to think. Many different scenarios went through my mind. None of them particularly good. I had a nasty feeling that I was going to be the main loser here, whatever the goings-on in Alistair's office were. God that bar of chocolate tasted good! I almost headed out to get another one but knew I'd be spotted by some eagle-eyed bitch who would have something to say about it. So instead I took to pacing around the office, which was tricky given its rather small dimensions. I got dizzy and had to sit down again. Christ, they were being an age! Whatever was going on?!

When Phil eventually returned, he shut the door (something we rarely did, except when facing a deadline and zero ideas) and took his seat. He didn't say a word to me. I stole a look; he was tapping his pencil on his pad, seemingly lost in thought. I couldn't read his face and decided it was probably best to wait for him to speak. Surely he'd have to say something soon? The silence was unbearable. But no, he continued to tap and stare so I left him to it and added a few more disturbing scenarios to my already over-active mind.

It wasn't till I got home that evening that I found out what had happened behind closed doors. And it certainly bore no resemblance to the wonderful things Charlie Rich had crooned about.

CHAPTER FORTY

Chris and I often got different trains home. Not by design you understand, just that it was difficult to coordinate our departures from the Agency so we rarely bothered, unless we were going somewhere together straight after work. That night Chris, unusually, beat me home. I walked into the kitchen to find him murdering a few carrots on the chopping board. Not wanting to startle him whilst he was fielding a sharp knife, I didn't say anything but went for a subtle re-arrangement of one of the kitchen chairs instead.

He turned around abruptly. "Hi."

Said with all the enthusiasm of a man encountering his soon-to-be ex-wife in a divorce court.

"Hiya!" I countered, way too brightly. "What's up, Doc? What's cooking?"

"Dunno. Just chopping stuff up at the moment. Salad probably. I bought some cold meats and cheeses."

"Sounds lovely. What can I do?"

"Nothing." He stuck his head in the fridge and re-emerged with a couple of colourful peppers.

I wasn't sure at this point how the evening was going to pan out, but I could see that at least we were going to eat well.

I didn't know what to do. Clearly something major had happened in Alistair's office, but I wasn't sure whether to broach the subject or wait until it was broached. What I desperately needed was a drink.

I sneaked into the dining room and, as quietly as possible, opened our drinks cabinet. I could hardly go into the kitchen for lemon and ice so I took a massive swig of vodka directly from the bottle. Not something I was in the habit of doing, but boy did it feel good! I stole a look behind me and took another mighty gulp.

Ready for battle now.

I wandered back into the kitchen just as Chris was setting our plates on the table. He gave me a rather omniscient look, which totally unnerved me, but I brazened it out.

"Looks fab Chris, thanks."

And indeed it did. Colourful, nutritious, filling and plenty of it.

We ate in silence for a good five minutes. I kept flicking looks at him, wondering if he was going to start the conversation, but his head was down and his focus remained entirely on his food.

I couldn't stand it any longer.

"So, what happened in Alistair's office then?"

He slowly raised his head, and my God did he look pissed off. "You mean your mate Phil didn't tell you?"

"No, my mate Phil did not tell me. He didn't say a word." I toyed with a piece of salami. "So are *you* going to tell me? Or not?"

He stabbed a slice of cucumber and studied it thoughtfully.

"Well I wouldn't quite call it the low point of my career to date, but it came pretty close." He shoved the cucumber into his mouth and speared another, whilst I waited patiently.

"Our dear, sweet MD informed me that I am no longer to work on the accounts of the clients that I apparently upset." In went the second slice of cucumber.

He didn't appear to be about to elaborate further, so I took a mouthful of my own food to give me time to think.

Still nothing, so I ventured, "Well Chris, I suppose-"

"Oh of course you're going to defend the decision! Thanks a lot, Sarah! Why can you never bloody support me?"

I was outraged and shocked. Bloody support him?? What the frigging hell had I been doing for the last few years?

"You don't even know what I was about to say."

"I can guess." He took a mouthful of water and stared at me. "That's not all."

"What's not all?"

"Phil is now looking after those clients who no longer, according to Alistair, wish to work with me. How do you like that? I suppose that makes you happy?"

This was so unfair. As usual, he was taking his rage out on me. Was any of it my fault? I didn't think so.

"None of this makes me happy, none of it. I'm gutted for you. It's horrible. And I'm stuck in the middle being married to you and working with Phil. How do you think that makes *me* feel?"

"Oh dear, I'm so sorry Sarah. Poor you." He got up from the table and cleared his plate away. I was still eating but had somehow lost my appetite.

"No need for the sarcasm, Chris. This is not easy for either of us. How…how did you react in Alistair's office to the news of Phil looking after those clients?" I had a feeling I knew the answer.

"Oh you know, argued the toss a bit but had to accept

177

it. I'm fucking annoyed about it but what can I do? Phil did his best to hide his delight at the news, but he couldn't quite conceal the smirk on his face. Bastard. Fucking bastard."

I couldn't really see how this was Phil's fault either. There was only one person to blame for this situation and that was the man who was currently banging plates and cutlery into the dishwasher. Shit. Here we go again. Another sodding hurdle to overcome.

Interestingly, I found out from Phil the next day, when he finally opened up to me about it, that Chris hadn't actually accepted the news with reasonable grace. On the contrary, he'd been incredibly angry, saying that Phil had always been after his job and he wasn't having it. In the end, when he realised there was absolutely nothing he could do about it, he capitulated with the words 'I'm watching you Phil. I'm watching you." Seems Phil felt quite intimidated, hence the vacant staring and tapping back in the office.

My life had become a complete nightmare. Becks was right; I should leave him. I should have left him a long time ago. We should never have got married. But if we split up it meant I would have to leave my job too! I certainly couldn't carry on working there. I loved my job. I loved the accounts I worked on and I enjoyed working with Phil, for all his quirks. Did I really have to change my whole life because I couldn't make our marriage work? What did I mean *I* couldn't make the marriage work?? What was I doing wrong exactly? Surely to God it was Chris who was ruining everything here? But he was ill. He had an addiction. Was that his fault? Oh sodding hell.

Chapter Forty-one

The next evening we had another counselling session after work. We'd pretty much managed to avoid each other during the day, which was quite an achievement given the size of the Agency's creative department. Chris certainly didn't come anywhere near our office and I surreptitiously checked out the communal coffee area, under-cover detective-like, before I ventured anywhere near. Apart from Phil elaborating on the events that took place in Alistair's office, he and I didn't discuss it.

I did wonder whether Chris might use our latest argument as an excuse to skip the counselling session, so I had to find out if he was still intending to go. That involved having some kind of conversation with him, which meant actively seeking him out at the end of the working day to gauge what the plan was. When I stuck my head around his door to rather timidly enquire as to his intentions, he answered with such normality- ('of course I'm coming to the session, I'll see you by the door downstairs in ten') that I thought I'd imagined the whole argument and awkwardness between us. He was some actor. Definitely missed his vocation in life.

And so we headed off, not quite hand-in-hand, but at

least on speaking terms, to our weekly meeting. We had a tacit agreement not to talk about the impending session on our way there. We never quite knew what questions we were going to be asked anyway, or what the other person was going to say, so there was no point discussing it ahead of time.

Seems I'd underestimated our counsellor, Jennifer. She was clearly better at her job than I'd previously given her credit for; she read our body language immediately.

"So tell me what's going on Sarah, what's happened between the two of you?"

Shit, why did she have to pick on me!

"Umm, well, we're not doing that great at the moment, actually."

"Tell me about it."

I looked at Chris but his focus was solely on the overly-patterned carpet. So I decided to go for it. After all, Jennifer had told me not to try and bury things or put an acceptable veneer on events, so I let her have it. I told her all about our disastrous visits to our respective parents (we'd touched on this at previous sessions but not gone into detail about them) and then I told her that Chris had returned to work after his enforced spell at home but that things were not good there. I didn't elaborate on what exactly the problem was – I surely had to leave something for her to question Chris about?

She did indeed turn her attention to Chris after I'd finished speaking. She asked him about the visits, why had they not been enjoyable and what had happened at work. He glossed over most of the problems of the parental visits by saying it was his fault because he'd wanted a drink. About the work situation, there was no way he was going to tell her what was going on there so he put on his usual act saying all

180

was well, nothing to see here…etc etc. She probed further, saying that I had indicated a problem and she'd like to hear from Chris what it was. Bit of a mistake on Jennifer's part there. No way was Chris going to respond to being treated like a naughty child. She looked at me, willing me to open up instead, but I just shrugged. I had to maintain some kind of solidarity with my husband.

So she returned to the visits and the fact that Chris was frustrated at not drinking and took it out on me. How did that make you feel, Sarah? Well how the fuck do you think it made me feel, Jennifer! But then she asked me if I felt guilty about Chris not drinking, did I feel responsible? I had difficulty answering that. In the end I said yes, I did feel a bit guilty.

Chris actually looked at me with some concern then.

"It's not your fault, Sarah. And it's not your problem. It's mine."

"Well thank you, but it is very much my problem too."

"How does that make you feel hearing Sarah say that, Chris?" Jennifer's inevitable interrogative input.

"Just great, Jennifer!" He paused, perhaps re-thinking his knee-jerk reaction. "It hurts me. It saddens me of course." His face fell as he lost a bit of bravado.

She attempted once more to question Chris about his childhood and his upbringing, imploring him to share things with us by saying that it might be the difference between him coming to terms with his addiction or never being able to deal with it. That frightened the hell out of me to hear those words, but still he wouldn't budge.

Her parting words were that I was to remember that, although I had no choice but to share in this problem of

181

Chris's, I was in no way to blame for it. I wasn't exactly sure how that was going to be of practical use to either of us, but I thanked her for the advice.

I really wasn't in the mood to go for our usual post-session meal and partake in our weekly mocking of Jennifer and her methods, but Chris – ever chameleon-like – clearly wanted to go. So off we trotted.

Generally I was quite happy to follow Chris's lead and have a good old laugh at the whole counselling thing, but this time I couldn't bring myself to go along with it. Instead I told Chris that I thought we should perhaps start taking it a bit more seriously if we wanted to help our situation. That maybe we should try listening to Jennifer's advice and even try actually following it. Maybe, just maybe, she knew what she was doing. He just grunted but didn't argue with me. Which was something I suppose.

I tried changing the subject then, but really we were running out of safe topics to talk about, so I was a bit stuck. Work was off limits; holidays; babies; our parents…what the hell was left? I pounced on the fact that the tiles were falling off the wall in our downstairs bathroom, so it clearly needed renovating and what colour did he fancy? Safe if a little boring, but at least we discovered that we could still find some common ground. Turned out we both liked the idea of a pink bathroom. Who knew?

CHAPTER FORTY-TWO

And so our life continued apace. It was OK for a while – stable you might even say – but boy was it boring. Something was not right. There was definitely trouble in paradise. Oh, we carried on as if everything was normal, as if we were living the standard life of a recently-married, young, professional couple. But we weren't. We were way too polite with each other, both of us seemingly wary of saying or doing the wrong thing and thereby upsetting the already precarious apple-cart. I had stopped drinking in front of Chris altogether, something I'd previously promised to do but had forgotten all about. This seemed both fair and unfair to me but I concluded that it was the best course of action. For the time being at least.

Chris continued going to his AA meetings but when I asked about them he was not very forthcoming with information. Just said he was doing what he had to do and he was managing it OK but didn't wish to discuss it. Counselling continued, but despite my pleas he still didn't seem to take it seriously or learn anything from it.

I, on the other hand, started to digest more of Jennifer's advice and began to notice a slight change in my ability to deal with Chris and the situation. Not a seismic shift of any description, but a change nonetheless.

Work, thank heavens, was very busy for the two of us. Chris seemed to have accepted the fact that he was no longer working on a couple of the accounts, but he gave Phil a wide berth where possible and was very short and offhand with him during any meetings or briefings. Phil took it well, I thought. He could have lorded it around the agency a bit, now that he was in charge of a couple of our clients' accounts, but he didn't. Probably out of respect for me. I was grateful for that.

So I suppose for a period of time, we threw ourselves into our jobs, spending more and more time at the agency and less and less time at home during the week. We didn't discuss it but I guess we both came to the conclusion independently that this was the best way to live. But it couldn't go on that way could it? It wasn't right. It wasn't normal. It wasn't a life.

I chatted to Becky about it.

"Becks, I know you're sick and tired of hearing about me and my failing marriage, but we seem to be entering a new phase now." We were, for once, drinking coffee together rather than alcohol.

"I'll always listen to you mate, you know that. And it's amazing how much better I can concentrate on your problems when we're sober! Not so much fun though, is it? What I wouldn't give to be thrown out of another wine bar with you right now!"

I laughed as memories of that hilarious night came flooding back. Then I remembered how I'd behaved towards Ed.

"Oh God Becks, I was so embarrassing with Ed wasn't I?! Christ whatever did he think of me? I was bloody stroking his face at one point!"

Becky laughed good-naturedly. "That was so funny. He didn't really say much about it the next day – you know what men are like!"

"But, ignoring the fact that I was fawning over my best mate's boyfriend, the difference between your relationship and mine really struck me that night. Yours is just natural. Mine...isn't."

"Yeah well, you have issues in yours don't you? I mean we have our issues too but they're kind of minor ones. Ones that we can deal with together. Your problem is much more serious."

"You could say that, yes. I've been thinking lately how boring our marriage is. We don't behave like normal people towards one another. It's like we – me in particular – are treading on eggshells and not engaging in a regular relationship. Do you know what I mean?"

Becky took a long slurp of her coffee. "I think so, yes, but I can't imagine it to be honest Sarah. Ed and I are so relaxed with each other. I'm completely myself with him and I think he is with me too. That's how it should be, shouldn't it?"

I put my head in hands momentarily before looking at her. "Yes, of course it should. We used to be like that, in the beginning. It was wonderful. I loved him so much and we were so happy. Now, I'm not sure I even love him anymore. Some days I do, some days I don't. I really don't know what to do. I want to make it work, I absolutely do, but I don't know if I can." I hung my head and played with the little packets of sugar on the table.

"God I wish I could wave a magic wand and make everything right for you. I don't know what to say because only you know what you want. He's still off the drink, is he?"

"Yes. Well as far as I can tell he is. I think I'd know wouldn't I? If he is drinking, he's doing a good job at keeping it a secret."

"So that's good. He's sticking to his promise."

"Yes but he's not happy. He says his life is boring without alcohol and even though he's been off it some time now, that thinking doesn't seem to have changed. So will it ever? I don't know."

"Maybe you should give it a time limit in your head Sarah. Say to yourself 'right I will do everything to make this marriage work and to make Chris happy, but I will only give it, say, another three months'. What d'you think?"

"Maybe, yeah. It's an idea anyway." I drained the last of my coffee and banged my mug down. "Yes, I think you're right, Becks. I need to do something like that otherwise this will just go on and on and I'll never be happy. Thanks mate." I gave her a tearful hug. "What would I do without you?"

"Go after my Ed probably!"

We both laughed again and I felt happy that, with Becky's help, I'd made some kind of decision. What I wouldn't have given at that moment to be going home to an Ed rather than a Chris.

CHAPTER FORTY-THREE

I faced the next few weeks with a little more fortitude than the previous weeks. I had a plan, a fallback if you will. I was still trying my best to make the whole thing work, but in my head I could hear Jennifer telling me this wasn't my fault and Becky telling me I deserved better. This gave me the resolve I needed to proceed with the strategy.

I'd decided to go with the length of time that Becks had suggested; three months. So I had about twelve weeks to save my marriage otherwise I was out of here. It didn't make me feel happy that my marriage could soon be over, but it did give me more of a focus and made me less anxious about the whole thing. The clock was ticking …

So what did I do exactly to try and save my marriage? Well nothing that I would get a medal for, to be honest. I just did more of what I'd been doing for the last few months. Suggesting social things for Chris and I to do at the weekends and occasionally on weeknights; talking to him about work in an attempt to get him creatively fired up. I was also more responsive in our counselling sessions and tried to persuade Chris to follow my lead.

For my own sanity, I kept busy at the Agency and

continued to meet up with Becky once a week. I was actually really enjoying work and we were up the walls with campaigns, so Chris and I both had good reason to work late most nights. I had stopped going to the pub with my work mates, because I knew Chris wouldn't come. I continued not to drink in front of him, which was bloody difficult, but I decided that it should be part of the 'Trying To Save My Marriage' plan. He never commented on the fact that I was no longer having a glass of wine with dinner or a vodka & tonic pre-dinner. I felt he could have met me halfway and shown his appreciation for what I was doing, but hey, maybe that was too much to hope for.

I was still working with our student James from time to time and to be entirely honest I should say that I really enjoyed his company. We continued to go to recording and dubbing sessions together and I found him very intuitive when it came to creative input, and also good fun. He was still a child for God's sake – 21 – but he was pretty self-assured, and rather handsome. I have to admit that I did flirt with him a little. Couldn't help myself. I guess I'm just made that way. I shouldn't have because I knew he fancied me. But I saw it as harmless. It never got out of hand; we only saw each other in daylight hours and never went drinking together. I don't suppose he had any desire to risk his position in the Agency by sleeping with the boss's wife anyway, so I reckoned we were on mutually safe, if flirtatious ground. Chris continued to make the odd remark about our relationship but I always answered by telling him not to be so silly.

And how was Chris during this three month trial, even though he wasn't actually aware that it was a three month trial? Pretty much the same. Everything I tried was more or less in vain. Oh sure, we went out on the weekends; we went cycling, we went to the cinema and we occasionally got together with friends. But he remained aloof, distant from me, just going through the motions rather than appearing to enjoy anything much. He continued to go shooting on Sundays with Geoff and the gang, and I had to assume that he still enjoyed that but of course we'd agreed not to discuss it. We even had sex sometimes too, which was when I felt closest to him of course. It was still good and I hoped that that might be the thing that saved our marriage. But it wasn't to be.

I felt unbearably sad at times. How had it come to this? What happened to the fun-loving, entertaining, adorable man that I'd married? How was it possible that alcohol could play such a big part in someone's life? Hell, even be the most important *thing* in someone's life? Fuck's sake, I couldn't get my head around that. I tried asking him again about his AA meetings but he just got angry saying that he was going and that was what I wanted wasn't it? Well yes Chris, but I was also hoping for some kind of *result*. Well done for attending them, if indeed you still were, but why weren't they and our counselling sessions helping? Rhetorical question of course, I couldn't actually ask him any of this because I knew what kind of response I'd get.

And so one month passed, and then another, with very little change in our lives apart from my newly-acquired skill of swigging secretively from a vodka bottle. Not something of which I was particularly proud, I have to say, but a necessity all the same. I swear that Chris knew I was doing it, but to his credit he said nothing.

I talked to Becky during this time of course, and reported

what I was doing, what I was trying to do and what I appeared to be failing to achieve. She was brilliant. She kept my spirits up and insisted that I was doing everything I could and that I was giving it my best shot. I couldn't have got through it without Becky's help, I was sure of that.

Towards the end of the third month, when it was clear to me that my attempts had failed, I began to wonder how on earth I was going to broach the subject of separation with Chris. I didn't want to go straight for divorce; there was still hope if we just separated. But separate we had to. I was determined to stick to my plan. My sanity and future happiness depended on it. But how to break it to Chris? Well, wouldn't you know, he saved me the bother.

Chapter Forty-four

Looking back, the way it happened was pretty goddamn surreal really. I mean there was absolutely no prior clue, no hint whatsoever that what happened that night was going to happen. It was bloody mad. There was me trying to work out how to tell my husband that I was leaving him, and wondering what the consequences of that might be for both of us, little knowing that the universe had bigger and more sinister plans in mind for the two of us.

As I said, I'd been working very hard the last few weeks leading up to 'the event'. Chris had too. We'd actually not seen much of each other, but when we were together I'd been doing my utmost to try and make our time fun and 'normal'. I'd failed though, in my book. Or rather Chris had failed to respond to my none-too-subtle attempts. So we were looking down the barrel of separation. Not that he knew this of course. Unless he had some kind of sixth sense...? I doubted it.

So on what turned out to be the last night of my marriage, and indeed the last night before my life changed irrevocably, I got home quite late from work. I had no idea what time Chris had left the office, I just knew I was one of the last to leave. Seems ironic now, but during my journey home I was actually trying to come up with exactly how I was going to handle this whole thing with him. It was a Friday and I'd decided to wait until Saturday to tell him. I had a short-term exit plan up my sleeve, in the form of Becky's couch. I didn't actually know who was going to move out. I wasn't sure that I wanted to remain in that house by myself, so I was hoping that Chris would stay put and I would find somewhere in London. How exactly I was going to pay for this 'somewhere' was an issue I hadn't quite resolved yet.

I opened the door to the house with a heavy heart and a head spinning with emotions. There was no sign of Chris and none of the usual culinary sounds coming from the kitchen. I called out to him. No reply. I threw my jacket over the banisters and dumped my bag in the hall.

Sauntering into the lounge, the first thing I noticed was something propped up against the settee at the far end of the room. I squinted at it. Shook my head. Couldn't be… Chris's rifle? What the fuck?? Why was it out of its cabinet? What was he doing with it on a Friday evening? The second thing I noticed filled me with equal apprehension. The drinks cabinet was open and there was a half empty bottle of whiskey on the counter.

I looked around but couldn't see Chris anywhere. I honestly didn't know what to do so I just stood at the end of the room, waiting. Waiting for God only knew what. I was actually ridged with fear. I don't think I could have moved if I'd wanted to. My brain simply wouldn't compute what my eyes were telling me. His rifle? Out of its cabinet? Why? Clear evidence of drinking? When he's not supposed to drink and had been off the booze for months now?

I couldn't come up with any kind of logical solution for this disturbing scenario. As I was about to leave the room in order to re-enter in the hope that my eyes were somehow deceiving me, Chris appeared, stealth-like, at the opposite end of the room. He literally slunk in, glass of whiskey in hand, and in a ludicrous scene that felt like something out of a film, proceeded to grip his other hand around the business end of his rifle.

I stared at him for what felt like ages, still unable to move.

"Chris," my voice was barely audible. "Chris – wha... what are you doing? What's going on?"

"Ahh what's going on, she says. Poor thing. Totally in the dark. All innocent like." He slugged back some more whiskey. My heart was beating so fast and so loudly that I swear he must have been able to hear it from where he stood.

"Chris, why is your rifle out?"

"Oh this? Just been cleaning it, Sarah. You know me, like to keep it shipshape for whenever I might need it." He shot me a look. A combination of a smirk and pure hate.

What the hell was he on about? He went shooting once a week and cleaned his gun briefly prior to each outing, as far as I was aware anyway.

"But enough of me Sarah, let's talk about YOU. Where've you been? What have you been up to I wonder?"

"Wo...working, Chris. As you know."

"Oh is that what you call it? Working? Well I suppose it is related to work in a way, but we both know what you've been doing, Sarah. You little slut."

Good God how much worse was this going to get? I was surely caught up in some kind of ghastly nightmare. This just wasn't happening.

"I don't know what you mean, Chris."

"DON'T YOU? REALLY?" He was shouting now but his position hadn't shifted. Nor had mine. If only I'd had the foresight to run out of the room and out of the house to Lucy and Geoff next door. But there's no saying what might have happened if I'd done that.

"You've been with your FUCKING TOYBOY! HAVEN'T YOU? Everyone knows, Sarah, you can't keep something like that a secret. Not in the workplace. Everyone knows that you're a little TRAMP!"

Christ all-fucking-mighty. Everyone knows?? There was nothing *to* know! Was there gossip about me? Had someone who was jealous of me been winding Chris up about James and I? He'd always had his suspicions, which I'd constantly had to allay, but maybe all he needed was for a third person to confirm those suspicions to him. Maybe he actually *wanted* to hear them so that, in some bizarre way, it would justify his actions? And now here he was, drunk, with his hand around a rifle and firm in the belief that his wife was an adulterer. Not a good situation, clearly.

However, even though I plainly needed to choose my next words carefully, I never for one minute thought that Chris would actually shoot me. I didn't feel in any danger. You may find that strange, given the evidence, but Chris was my husband. He loved me. He wouldn't shoot me. He couldn't.

"Chris, it's simply not true – please, you have to believe me. I haven't even been working with James today, I've been finishing the Trebor ad with Phil. Phone him…ask him if you don't believe me."

"Oh yes, of course I'm going to fucking phone PHIL.

That gobshite isn't going to tell me the truth. He's your mate, 'course he's gonna stick up for you. You lying little fucking SLUT!"

"That's just not fair, Chris! How many times do I have to tell you? I'm NOT having an affair with James! Why do you insist on thinking that? What's wrong with you?"

"What's wrong with me? Well, let's start with the fact that I'm married to an adulterous bitch! A bitch who thinks she's so much better than me because she's won so many fucking awards! You and Phil, grinning away, clapping each other on the back, rubbing my sodding nose in it!"

"Jesus Christ, Chris!"

"Oh and I'm also married to a bitch who stopped me drinking. But does the bitch like a drink herself? Does she go out and get legless with her stupid little friend whenever she feels like it?" He banged his glass down on the counter and started pacing up and down, still holding the rifle. "Yes she fucking does!"

I couldn't believe the unending venom he was heaping on me. It was all so unreasonable, and I just couldn't let him get away with it.

"That is completely unfair, Chris. I've tried so hard to help you, to make our marriage work."

"Making me go to bloody AA meetings? Dragging me to boring counselling sessions? Is that your idea of how a marriage works? YOU'VE RUINED MY LIFE SARAH!"

Wow. A conversation-stopper if ever I'd heard one. But I had to defend myself.

"Ruined your life? You bastard! I've been trying to help you! Look at you! Look at the state you're in because you can't take your drink! You're an alcoholic Chris, admit it!"

And that was it. That was what tipped him over the edge. Before I realised what was happening, he'd grabbed the rifle with both hands, aimed it at me and pulled the trigger. Twice.

I remember hearing him shout 'YOU MADE ME DO THIS YOU FUCKING BITCH!' I was conscious of a huge surge of pain as I fell from the impact of the bullets.

Then only blackness.

CHAPTER FORTY-FIVE

So that is the sad story of how I came to be sitting in my hospital room, waiting for my surprisingly non-judgemental parents to come and collect me. I was to go home with them for a couple more weeks of recuperation.

With the benefit of that wonderful commodity hindsight, it was obvious to me that I had been a complete and utter idiot. The writing on the wall could not have been more conspicuous. I don't mean that Chris would inevitably end up shooting me, but that he was never going to accept a life without alcohol. Becky had tried to tell me of course. Several times. Why oh why did I not listen to my mate? Because love is blind I guess, and possibly deaf too. I didn't want her to be right and so I made up my own narrative and followed that for as long as I could, oblivious to what was going on in front of my very eyes.

I'd had nothing but time over the past few weeks to think about everything. Once my initial pain and discomfort had eased somewhat, I regularly found myself going over and over certain events and conversations in my head. I experienced several different moods; denial, anger, depression etc. Similar to the various stages of grief. Or so my counsellor told me. I was assigned a lovely man who came to see me twice a week and I must say I found him very helpful. He was better than Jennifer – the counsellor Chris and I had been seeing. Or maybe I was just a bit more receptive, I don't know. Anyway, with his diligence and perseverance we managed to reach the 'acceptance' phase, and so I was deemed cured. I suppose I *had* accepted the fact that my husband had shot me. But I hadn't really accepted *why* he'd shot me. Oh sure, he was an alcoholic, I knew that. But was that a reason? I mean how many alcoholics shoot their spouses? Actually I had no idea but it had to be a fairly low percentage, surely.

The 'acceptance' phase had seemed a long way off when I first opened my eyes in the hospital. I didn't know where I was or what had happened. I just knew that my sister and Mum & Dad were sitting around my bed, and that Mum was crying quietly. What was Caroline doing there? Thought she was on a Kibbutz or something. And why was Mum crying? I asked them what was going on. Slowly, as Dad spoke to me in his wonderful, soothing tone, my memories were reawakened.

Seemingly Chris had dialled 999 and asked for an ambulance to be sent to the house. So the man wasn't all bad then, was he? He didn't leave me there to bleed to death on our new carpet. He then fled though (not a great look) and was later found hiding out at his mate Dan's house. Desperate Dan to the rescue, of course. When the paramedics arrived, I had bled a lot but my injuries – although quite severe – were not life-threatening. One pellet to my shoulder, one to my thigh. At least he'd managed to avoid my heart and my head. I wondered if that had been deliberate or was he just a lousy shot? I intended to ask Geoff if I ever saw him again.

Dad also told me – get this – that Chris had pleaded self-defence. Said that I was angry and attacking him and that of course he didn't mean to do what he did it just happened… blah…blah…blah. I looked horrified as Dad explained this, but he reassured me that no one – including the police – believed him for one minute. I tried to say something but he said I was to rest and that we had plenty of time to talk. It made me cry, of course. My Dad had suddenly become my hero.

A couple of days' later, Becks came to see me. Poor girl was in a state, crying and trying her best to hug me whilst taking care not to hurt me. I cried buckets with her too. I said how sorry I was that I hadn't listened to her, what a good friend she was to me and how I didn't deserve her. This made her cry even more, which in turn made me cry even more. The nurse came in and started berating Becky for upsetting me. Poor Becks. Getting kicked out of hospital would have been a new one. If it had been any other given situation, we'd have laughed like hell about that.

I suddenly thought about our house. I wasn't there, Chris wasn't there. Was it unlocked? Was the front door wide open even? Becky was able to reassure me that she'd (of course she had) driven down to check it out and had spoken with Geoff and Lucy, who had a spare key. They had made sure everywhere was locked up and were keeping an eye on it. Obviously that was after the police and forensics had done their bit. I asked her how Geoff and Lucy had taken the news. She said that they were clearly hugely shocked. Geoff felt tremendously guilty because he'd introduced Chris to shooting and had suggested he get his own rifle. It wasn't his fault, I knew that. How could he have known that Chris would end up using the rifle on me? Although, that said, I did harbour a little bit of annoyance towards him and several 'what ifs?' crossed my mind, but my counsellor – the dear man – soon knocked that out of me.

The first week or so in hospital went by in a bit of a blur; a few visitors – family, Becky and one other friend only – pain, medication, procedures and more pain. The second week though, brought me not only less pain but some much-needed clarification when I received a surprise visitor in the form of Jane, Chris's sister.

Chapter Forty-six

At first, I thought I was surely dying. What the hell was Jane doing here, all the way from America? But she soon reassured me that I was actually quite a bit better (according to the medical staff) and that I was not about to give up the ghost.

For some reason, I felt embarrassed that Jane was there, at my bedside. Embarrassed that she had to see for herself the awful injuries I'd received at the hands of her brother.

"Jane," I croaked. "I can't believe you're here. It's good to see you."

"You too, Sarah, only I wish the circumstances were different."

I looked away.

"God, I don't know what to say. The doctor just told me that you're doing well, but…Christ almighty Sarah. My own brother…"

I was about to say something to comfort her, even though I was the patient here, but she quickly disabused me of any notion that she required consolation.

"Look, I had to come, of course. This isn't about my distress, it's about you and what Chris did to you."

I blanched when she said his name.

"I couldn't believe it when Mum rang me, she…"

"Oh God, your poor Mum – how is she? Must be in bits. Much like myself…" I was pleased that I hadn't entirely lost my sense of humour.

"She is, Sarah, she is. I'm staying with her. She's pretty inconsolable. It's awful, but she has to face facts."

"Where's…where's Chris at the moment?" I was suddenly concerned for my safety. Wondered if he might try and find me and finish the job.

"He's in custody. They didn't grant him bail."

"Oh. Right. Have you seen him?"

"No, not yet. Not sure if I want to actually, but I'll take Mum anyway."

We sat in silence for a few minutes, neither of us sure what to say next.

After a while, Jane said "Do you know why he did this, Sarah? I mean what prompted it?"

"Well he was drunk. And for some reason he had his rifle out of the cabinet. He thought I was having a fling with a guy from work and was shouting all sorts of abuse at me and not listening to anything I said. He seemed to be blaming me for everything that had gone wrong in his life. Then he just shot me. I wasn't, by the way."

"You weren't what?"

"Having an affair."

"Even if you were, it's hardly a good enough reason to shoot you is it?"

"Well, no."

"But why did he think you were having this affair?"

"Because of my relationship with this young guy I was mentoring at work. We got on well and I do think he fancied me, but nothing ever happened. He's only a kid! Chris got it

202

into his head that something was going on. I kept on telling him he was wrong. I guess I didn't realise how much it must have been eating away at him."

"This isn't your fault Sarah, none of this is your fault. You know that, right?"

"Yeah, my counsellor has drummed that into me."

"Good."

Another short silence during which I stared out of the window and thought briefly about the Agency and how the gossips there must have gone into overdrive.

"When did he start drinking again? 'Cos when I was visiting, he was off the booze – remember?"

"He'd been off it a while actually. He was really trying hard." I spun my head round then, a little too quickly it has to be said as it made me a bit dizzy, and looked Jane in the eye.

"Did you know about his drink problem, Jane?"

She sighed and shifted her weight in the chair.

"Sarah, Sarah, I have to tell you the sad story of our family. It might help make some sense of all of this, although I'm not sure it will bring you much comfort."

I stared at her, willing her to go on.

"Our Dad was an alcoholic. Our childhood was pretty shit. I remember more than Chris of course, being older, but he was affected too. Dad held down a job OK but he was pretty much an absent father. Most of his free time was spent in the pub. Actually, it he'd stayed absent it would've been fine. It was when he came home that the trouble started. He'd verbally abuse us, throw things around the house and occasionally physically abuse Mum."

"Oh my God, that's awful, Jane!" I adjusted my position in the bed so that I could see her better.

"Yes it was. But Mum was in denial. I was too young to be of any real help to her, but I could see what was going on all right. When I asked her why she let Daddy hurt her, she just said he didn't mean to and that he'd had a bad day at work. Or something like that."

I let that sink in. "Did she ever get the police or social services involved?"

"She was too scared. She just carried on with life and did her best to protect us."

"What happened to him?"

"Well, eventually, when I was about ten and Chris nearly seven, Mum's sister – Aunty Claire? – staged a daring intervention. She knew from Mum that Dad was working away for a couple of days so she drove over and insisted Mum packed up what she needed for the three of us and moved out there and then."

"And your Mum went?"

"She had no choice really. Aunty Claire simply bullied her into it, saying that the situation could not go on any longer and that she should think of the children if not herself."

"So where did you all go?"

"She'd sorted out a Council house not far from where she lived and we went there. Aunty Claire had connections apparently, and she pulled a few strings for us."

"And what about your Dad?"

"Aunty Claire wrote to him and told him that we'd moved. She said he was not to try and contact us or ever see us again."

"Bloody hell. How did he take that?"

"I don't know. I only ever asked Mum about him once. I wanted to know if we'd see him again and she said 'No love, it's for the best.' I didn't really care because I didn't like him."

"What about Chris? How did he react?"

"Ahh well, that's a different story."

Just at that point, a nurse entered my room and told Jane that she had to leave. Talk about timing.

CHAPTER FORTY-SEVEN

I can tell you that I had an extremely restless night. The nurses said that I was muttering all sorts of things in my sleep, which was a surprise to me because it felt as though I'd had no sleep at all. My head was full of all manner of thoughts, but I had to hear the end of Jane's story before I could begin to make any sense of them.

The morning dragged interminably until finally the clock struck two and Jane re-entered my room. With the niceties and handing over of yet more grapes out of the way, we resumed business.

"So Jane, you were going to tell me about how Chris reacted to being taken away from your Dad", I prompted.

"Erm, yes. Well, like I said, Chris was younger than me so he didn't witness as much of the abuse as I did, nor was he on the receiving end of it quite so much."

"Did your Dad spare Chris or was it that he just wasn't there mostly when it happened?"

"A bit of both really. Whether it was in recognition of some kind of misplaced male bonding or whether it was due to Chris's age, I don't know, but yes, Dad did seem to spare him a bit. Also Chris was generally asleep when he came home from the pub so he didn't see as much. I used to lie awake waiting for him to come home sometimes, in the hope that I could somehow protect Mum. Never could of course, I was just shouted at and told to go back to bed."

Jane paused and looked away. I felt sorry for her that she had to relive these awful memories.

"Are you OK, Jane? We don't have to do this if you don't want to."

"Oh we do Sarah. You need to know the truth."

She shook herself and continued.

"So anyway, we went to our new house, courtesy of Aunty Claire. Everything was fine for a while. We settled in and got to know our new surroundings. We had to change schools of course so that was a little unnerving, but we were still very young so we adapted fairly quickly. Or at least I did."

"Can't have been easy for any of you. How was your Mum?"

"She was strange really. I think, bizarrely, that she resented Aunty Claire for taking us away from Dad. Even though she said reassuring things to Chris and me, I heard her crying in her bedroom sometimes, and even saying Dad's name over and over."

"But then she still loved him didn't she?"

"Guess so. She never fully accepted he was as bad as he was. She was blinkered. You know you hear about women like that and you wonder how on earth they can stay in an abusive relationship?"

"Yep." I was thinking of myself. I surely fell into that category.

"They think that they are somehow to blame, and they also seem to think that each time it happens it won't happen again."

Bingo.

I nodded.

"Well that was Mum I s'pose. But I need to tell you about Chris."

I pulled the covers up under my chin and waited with some apprehension.

"He never settled at the new school. He made a couple of friends all right, but he was always in and out of trouble. He was a clever boy but he never bothered to try very hard – except in English, which you're probably not surprised to hear. He knew he was really good at that and took great pleasure in shining during lessons and belittling some of the other pupils."

"Nice."

"Yes, well that turned out to be one of his more endearing qualities. He became a nasty bully and was suspended from school several times, and eventually expelled."

"He never told me any of this!"

"No, I guess not. He probably wasn't that proud of it."

"So what happened to him?"

"He was in his final year at primary school by the time he was expelled, so Mum didn't bother to look for another school for him. She just kept him home until it was time to start secondary school."

"But how did she manage to find a school to take him?"

"He went to the same one as me. Mum and Aunty Claire spoke to the principal to explain the situation – you know about Dad and moving and all that – and about how Chris was obviously upset by the changes in his life. I don't know exactly what they said obviously, but seemingly the school was happy to take him on."

"And how did that go?"

"He was fine for the first couple of years. Mainly because he was a small fish in a big pond I think, rather than the other way round as it had been. Several pupils in his class had older brothers or sisters at the school so if he'd caused any trouble there would have been some form of retribution I feel."

"Did he make friends and keep up with the school work?"

"Yep – seems he did quite well in class generally and he made a couple of good buddies, yes. But…"

"I somehow felt there was a but coming…" I sat up a little straighter.

"Yes, well apparently he started drinking. At about the age of thirteen."

"Jesus. I didn't know he'd started that early. Did your Mum know?"

"I think she did. She must have. I didn't really cotton on to it all until he was about fourteen or fifteen, which is when it became more of a problem."

"Right. What happened?"

"Erm, well he started abusing Mum and me. Verbally, not physically. The smallest thing would set him off and he'd just shout at us. He got incredibly angry sometimes, it was quite frightening."

She looked at me and we both fell silent.

"I know he did that to you too didn't he Sarah? I remember what happened at the end of your wedding day."

Tears were sliding uninvited down my cheeks.

"Did it happen again? Did he abuse you?"

"Yes," I managed to breathe.

"I'm so sorry, Sarah. I should have warned you about

him before your wedding. I should have talked to you. God if only I had, things might be very different now."

"No Jane, it's not…"

Jane got up and started pacing around the room.

"It's just that I hadn't seen Chris much since moving to America, obviously, and I simply assumed that he was over it. That he'd acquired some kind of self-control. I should have known better."

"It's not your fault. Of course it's not. I should have left him the first time he did it to me. Which was actually before our wedding. I'm like your Mum. I thought it was my fault for a long time, and each time it happened I was sure it wouldn't happen again."

"You loved him Sarah, anyone could see that."

"Yes but you have no sympathy for the way your Mum dealt with your Dad, and she loved him – so why do I get a pass here?"

"I don't know. But you mustn't blame yourself. I was a child when everything was going on with Mum and Dad, but I understand a lot more about everything now. Why people do things they do, or don't do things that might seem obvious to bystanders."

She sat down again.

"How did your Mum react when all this was going on?" I asked.

"Ignored it mainly. Brushed it under the carpet. Nothing to see here – he's fine."

I was shocked.

"Really?"

"Oh yes. She said that we had to cut him some slack because he'd grown up without a father. That it wasn't his fault. Life was difficult for him but he would be all right with our help. Blinkered, just like she was with Dad."

"Did the school know about his drinking?"

"No. It mainly took place after school or on the weekends. Amazingly he kept up with his schoolwork pretty well. He was cute, you see, didn't want to rock the boat there because he knew that would mean big trouble. And he knew he could get away with appalling behaviour at home without any repercussions. He was a little shit, Sarah. A charmer, true, but a little shit all the same."

That certainly resonated with me.

"Aunty Claire tried to intervene a few times, suggesting we should get help for him, but Mum flatly refused. On one occasion, we actually said to Mum that he was just like his father. Red rag to a bull. She flew into a rage and there was a massive argument. She threw Aunty Claire out and told her to leave us alone. Then she turned on me, started shouting that I should be more supportive of my own brother."

I must admit I had trouble envisaging Chris's Mum shouting at anyone, never mind her own daughter. She seemed such a timid thing.

Right on cue, Nurse Veronica arrived and told us time was up. To be honest, I was relieved. I felt completely overwhelmed by everything Jane had told me. And she wasn't done yet.

211

Chapter Forty-eight

I knew I had to speak to someone. And of course there was only one person that could be.

"Becks – can you talk?"

"'Course babe – how are you?"

"Not good, Becky…"

"Why, what's happened? Tell me Sarah!"

"Oh nothing physical – I'm doing fine in that regard. Well apart from the fact that I've still got this wretched catheter in and it's driving me mad. And none of your jokes about how handy it might be on a night out…!"

Becky laughed. "I'm sorry that you still have to put up with that – it will be gone soon though yeah?"

"Apparently, yes."

"So what's the problem?"

I told her about Jane's visits and everything she'd said to me. As much as I could remember anyway. It all came out in a bit of a rush and Becks had a hard time making sense of some it. She managed to get the gist though.

"That happens so often Sarah, the abused becomes the abuser."

"Except that he wasn't really abused, according to Jane, he escaped most of it."

"Yeah, but he witnessed it at times didn't he and something obviously rubbed off on him."

"Was I a complete and utter twat Becky?"

"How d'you mean? I'd say yes to that, but really it needs qualifying…"

"Ha ha. Very funny. I mean why did I stay with him? Why couldn't I see that he was never going to change?"

"You loved him Sez, and you wanted to give him every possible chance of changing. Didn't you? And, to be fair to the fucking bastard, he did try. He gave up drinking for a good while right?"

"Yes, he did. But he became boring, didn't he? I was never enough for him. He needed the drink. Honestly Becky, everything is just going round and round in my head. I can't make sense of it. I'm going mad here. Why couldn't I see what he was like? Why did I stay with him?"

"Hindsight is a wonderful thing, hun. You didn't want to give up on your marriage. You wanted the man back that you fell in love with. Sez, you couldn't have done more to try and change him and make your marriage work. You threw everything at it and, in the end, you paid a big price. What he did to you was inexcusable and in no way your fault. You know that now, don't you? We've talked about it?"

"We sure have, and I've talked about it ad infinitum with my psychotherapist. Or analyst or whatever he's called – I never know the difference."

"Jonathan. I met him once when I was visiting. Rather cute I thought! Is he single?"

"Funnily enough Becky, that has yet to come up in our conversations together. But, yes, he is rather cute now you come to mention it…Becks, why did I not listen to you? You told me so many times to leave him, that he was no good, that I deserved better."

"Look mate, I was only doing what a good friend should do. You'd do the same for me. I just didn't like the way he treated you sometimes and I felt that his drinking was always going to be a problem. But my God girl, if I ever thought for one minute he'd end up doing what he did to you, I would have been there in a flash, dragging you out of that house, kicking and screaming if necessary. It upsets me so much Sarah, what he did to you. I can't even…"

Poor Becky, she trailed off and I could hear she was crying. Which started me off too, of course.

"Becks, don't," I wailed.

Cue Nurse Veronica again. I swear that woman stationed herself permanently outside my door so that she could time her entrances to a tee. She was not happy to see me in tears and guessed immediately that I was talking to 'that friend of mine' again.

"Gotta go Becks – talk soon."

Chapter Forty-nine

After another restless night and a long, long morning, Nurse Happy showed Jane into my room again. Did the woman never have a day off?

"She's very tired today – don't exhaust her too much". She glared at Jane as she closed the door on us.

"She must have skipped the 'bedside manner' classes don't you think?" Jane sat down next to my bed.

"Don't get me started…"

"Where was I, Sarah? I haven't told you about his conviction yet have I?"

Well that wasn't the opener I was expecting. Good God, how much worse was this going to get?

"Err no Jane, I don't believe you have."

"He beat someone up and was done for assault."

"What?? Who? What happened?"

"One of his classmates. It happened after school, but there were quite a few witnesses. The other guy pressed charges."

"Was he badly hurt? The other guy I mean." I didn't give a toss about Chris.

"Pretty bad, yeah, but he recovered OK."

"What happened to Chris?"

"He got a fine, that's all. But it was a conviction so he has a criminal record."

"And he was chucked out of school presumably?"

Jane took a sip from her luke-warm tea. "Well no, he wasn't. Some loophole apparently, because it happened outside of school hours and not on the premises."

I stared at her. "Really? That doesn't seem right."

"I think a lot of pupils and parents were miffed by it. Not happy at all. He was on a warning all right though, one more strike and he was out. Nevertheless he got to stay on to take his A Levels."

"Must have been a difficult time for him. Not that I'm feeling sorry for the bastard. It *should* have been a difficult time for him."

My mind was wandering and trying to locate something that was tantalisingly just out of my reach.

"He pretty much kept his head down after that and concentrated on his school work. He was determined to get into Uni to do his English degree."

"And that was allowed too? With a criminal record?"

"Seems so, yes. I never questioned it at the time actually."

That was it! Criminal record!

"Jane – Chris owned a rifle. You know, the one that was in the house? The one that he…that he shot me with."

"I know, Sarah, yes."

"But how was he able to get a licence for a gun when he had a criminal record?"

Jane looked at me and shook her head.

"He shouldn't have been able to should he?"

"Did you ever actually see the licence?"

"No, but…Geoff, our neighbour, organised it all for him."

My brain was working overtime. Did he have a licence? Maybe Geoff owned it? If so, what excuse did Chris give for not taking on the licence himself? No wonder Geoff was feeling bloody guilty! Christ almighty!

"He should never have owned that gun. That gun should not have been in our house! And if that gun hadn't been in our house, then I wouldn't be here in this sodding hospital!" I couldn't help my loud, self-pitying sobs.

Jane rushed to comfort me.

"I know, Sarah, I know. It's all wrong. It's all horribly wrong." She cradled me, both of us rocking from side to side. Nurse Veronica arrived…

"Right, that's enough! Out! My patient needs to rest. Step away from the bed!"

I don't believe she actually said those last few words, but I like to think she might have done.

Jane dutifully released me from her grasp and stood up.

"I can't come tomorrow, Sarah, I'm taking Mum to see… well to see Chris. But I'll call you in the morning, OK?"

I nodded and attempted a weak smile.

She glared at Nurse Veronica as she made her way to the door. "Look after her."

Nurse Veronica, to her credit, remained silent but judging by her body language I didn't fancy Jane's chances of getting a cup of tea next time she visited.

CHAPTER FIFTY

I didn't see Jane again as she had to return to the States sooner than anticipated, but she did call me as promised. She filled in the missing years for me. Not much to say really except that he drank his way through Uni and several girlfriends, somehow managed to get a decent degree and then set his sights on advertising. One of the few businesses that would tolerate a drink habit, I suspected. Or one where you could successfully hide a drink habit maybe. Unless you did something stupid like shoot your wife of course.

Their Mum continued to ignore his obvious alcoholic tendencies and refused to ever discuss it with Jane. Jane was never that close with either her mother or brother, a situation that her post-Uni move to America did nothing to improve. She kind of washed her hands of him – and her mother to a certain extent – and I could tell she was feeling very guilty about that now. It seemed that a lot of people close to me were suffering from one form of guilt or another over this lamentable situation. Some justified in my view. But really there was only one person to blame in this whole sorry saga. The man who'd had his finger on the trigger. Twice. Though I did wonder what was going through his Mum's head currently and ventured a question to Jane:

"What has your Mum said about all of this, Jane? Does she feel any remorse for not trying to do anything about his drinking problem when he was younger?"

A long silence at the other end of the phone.

"Jane?"

"I was hoping you weren't going to ask me that."

"Well, I'm afraid I just did."

"She feels no remorse. I actually asked her that and she was indignant at the very thought. She's in pieces about Chris."

"What about me? Has she spared a thought for me at all?"

"Sarah, I…I don't quite know how to say this. It's awful and I'm so embarrassed because she's my mother."

"It's OK Jane. I can take it." Said with a bravado I didn't truly feel.

"She blames you. Says this whole thing was your fault."

Whoa! Well I wasn't expecting that. They say blood is thicker than water all right but was the woman really that stupid? Fucking deplorable.

I eventually found my voice. "Good God, Jane. I can't believe that. How exactly was it my fault?"

"I know, Sarah, I know. I'm so sorry. It's awful. She said that, um, she said you never made him happy. You stopped him from drinking and being the man he was. You drove him to do it."

I was too shocked to cry but even so a strange sound escaped my lips. I tried to muffle it lest Nurse Veronica came rushing in with a sedative or something.

"We had a huge argument about it, soon after I got here.

I was so angry with her. I said things to her that a daughter should never say to a mother, and I don't regret them. I should have left there and then and gone back home. But I wanted to see you. And I couldn't quite bring myself to abandon her completely; she's so weak and frail at the moment. She doesn't have anyone else. Aunty Claire washed her hands of her. She heard about the shooting of course and couldn't take Mum's defence of Chris."

I tried to absorb all of this. I felt doubly betrayed. First by the son, now by the mother. There was something else I needed to know from Jane though.

"You went to see Chris yesterday, didn't you?"

"We did, yes. I wasn't going to go in with Mum but she couldn't manage it on her own. Also, I wanted to see the bastard to tell him what I thought of him."

That cheered me up a little.

"And...how was it? I mean the visit – how did it go?"

"He's a broken man, Sarah. I was all fired up, expecting him to be nonchalant and defensive. I really thought I might punch him in the face the minute I saw him. But he's broken. Having a rough time in there too, from some of the other inmates."

I almost felt sorry for him.

Jane must have read my mind.

"But don't feel sorry for him, Sarah – I don't. He committed a heinous crime and he deserves no sympathy. He got it from Mum of course, which was nauseating to watch, but he brushed her away. He didn't want to hear her platitudes, had no time for her compassion."

"Is he...did he say he was sorry for doing it?"

"He did. A hundred times over. If he could take that day

220

back and start all over again…etc etc. Wanted to know how you were too, of course."

I had to end the conversation. I thanked Jane for coming to see me and wished her a safe return journey. She promised to keep in touch and said she'd be over again soon.

I felt marginally cheered at the thought of Chris being sorry and repentant. He'd clearly got over his stance of having shot me in self-defence. I had no sorrow though for his 'broken man' status. That he deserved. But a second, more powerful emotion overtook me. The absolute needlessness of the act. It shouldn't have happened. It was totally avoidable. Oh yes, Chris, if only we could both take that day back and start all over again.

CHAPTER FIFTY-ONE

So…I was getting out of this place and going to Mum and Dad's for a couple of weeks. Back to my old bedroom. I was actually looking forward to it. I would have more space and freedom and would be my own boss to a certain extent. Shame to be leaving Nurse Veronica though.

Without a doubt Mum was going to spoil me and fuss over me, but I felt I could take a bit of that. Dad was there to temper everything. And my long-lost sister Caroline was even staying for a week or so too.

I was to have regular visits from the physio, to check on my improvement and to make sure that I was doing my prescribed daily exercises. I'd been signed off from psychiatric care so sadly I wouldn't be seeing the lovely Jonathan again. But I had his number – 'just in case', he'd said. Just in case of what, I wondered. I had a relapse? I wanted to meet him for a drink? He did hold onto my hand rather longer than necessary when he bade me his last farewell, but I really wasn't in any kind of fit state yet to contemplate a relationship – never mind one with my psychiatrist! Becky, no doubt, would have had different notions.

The only cloud on the otherwise relatively bright horizon was the impending trial.

Once home and back in my comfortingly familiar bedroom, I realised that somebody had brought a few of my clothes and belongings over from our house. My suspicions were confirmed by Caroline; Becky, of course. My favourite ornaments were on the bedside table, along with a few books. The wardrobe and chest of drawers were full of my clothes. Becks really was one in a million.

Although it was nice to be back at my parents' house, it also felt strange at first to be out of hospital. I was a little nervous initially. Would I be all right? What if I had a problem with something? It had been reassuring to have knowledgeable staff on call should you need it, even in the guise of Nurse Veronica. I did feel OK though. I had my regular medication to take, my physio exercises to do and I knew that Mum would be feeding me up a storm. Mum was never the best cook but, having experienced hospital food for so long, I was really looking forward to one of Mum's shepherd's pies…soggy potato topping notwithstanding.

I soon settled in and was pleased to be up and out of bed for most of the day. I still needed a rest each afternoon but was able to get out in the garden and walk a bit. Also I was finally able to concentrate well enough to actually get stuck into a good book again.

Mum and Dad were brilliant. They didn't ask me too much about anything, didn't delve too deep into my state of mind. They just took care of me and watched out for me. Caroline and I had a few chats. It was lovely – we really became close. Closer than we'd ever been in fact. She told me all about her life on the kibbutz and that she'd left immediately when she

223

heard about what had happened to me. I expressed guilt that she'd had to leave on my account, but she said it was the best thing she'd ever done! Didn't regret it one bit and didn't miss it – or her weird-sounding boyfriend there – in the slightest. I didn't feel I could comment on a bad partner choice.

I told Carrie all about my relationship with Chris. I went into detail about all the awful drinking episodes and arguments and how I'd tried so hard to get him off the booze. She was a good listener; totally non-judgemental and full of empathy. We talked about her failed marriage too, which had kind of petered out rather than going with a bang like mine did. Or indeed a double bang, if you want to be specific. I discovered a new-found respect and fondness for my big sis and, like I said, we really bonded. She said the same sort of things that Becky said to me, but in a less dramatic way. Becks was always one for the drama!

Talking of the devil, she was on the phone to me daily and came over to visit with Ed at the weekend. It was so lovely to see them both. I was always fond of Ed – he was such a sweetheart and I could see the pain in his eyes when he told me how sorry he was for what had happened. Would I ever find an Ed? Would I ever trust a man again was probably a more pertinent, although equally rhetorical, question right now.

Becky and I had great chats and it was good to laugh with her again. Particularly with the knowledge that Nurse Veronica wouldn't appear at any moment and put a stop to our fun. Becks told me that she had been looking out for a flat for me to move into in London, once I felt ready to do so. She wanted to find one close to her so that we could see each other all the time, she said. Even though that was a lovely thought, I felt very apprehensive about living on my own. I wasn't sure I could cope – not in a physical or domestic sense but a mental one. However, Caroline came to the rescue. Seemingly she and Becky had been discussing it. Carrie said she wanted to move to London too, so the plan was for us to share a place. Sounded perfect to me – and to my parents of course. I was well and truly being looked after by my wonderful family and friends. Just the final hurdle to get over now…

I'd tried to put it to the back of my mind, and to some extent I was successful, but as the trial date approached I became more and more uneasy.

Mainly because I'd see his face again.

CHAPTER FIFTY-TWO

There was no requirement for me to attend the whole trial. I had to give evidence at some stage of course, but outside of that I didn't have to be there if I didn't want to. I did want to though. Except 'want' is perhaps a big word here. I felt compelled to be there. I had to see him, to hear what he had to say. Even though I simultaneously dreaded it.

I scanned the courtroom on the first day and immediately caught sight of Chris's Mum in the front row. Our eyes locked and she veritably scowled at me before looking away. I was shocked. Even given what Jane had told me about her mother, I hadn't prepared myself for that kind of reaction. Becky, my dear Becky, had caught the look too and before I could stop her, she was on her feet and marching across the courtroom. Proceedings hadn't yet got under way so there was no one to shout 'Order!' at her. I watched fascinated as she bent her head towards Chris's Mum and gave her what appeared to be a true Becky-style mouthful. I couldn't hear what she was saying but I saw Iris recoil and revert to the timid woman I always knew her to be. God, she was weak! And pathetic. Becks stalked back to her seat and gave me a smile and a discreet thumbs up.

I wanted to hug her. At that very moment though, we were instructed to 'All rise!'

I glanced along our row. Mum, Dad, Caroline and Becky. My support team. The judge strode in and we were directed to resume our seats. I was pleased to see that the judge was male. I felt he wouldn't be taken in by Chris's charms. Or his pools of blue.

Once we were all seated again, a door opened and I watched with mounting trepidation as the prison officers escorted the offender into the room. My plaster-free hand flew involuntarily to my face. Dad placed a comforting arm around me and Becky shot me a look of concern.

Chris's shoulders were slumped and his head was down. He looked thin. He looked wretched. A broken man, as Jane had rightly surmised. I couldn't take my eyes off him. I went through a rapid series of emotions – if it hadn't been for Dad pinning me down with his arm, I think I might have fled.

The judge was now asking him to confirm his full name. Chris mumbled something inaudible and was instructed to look up and to speak louder. He raised his head a little and our eyes met. Those beautiful pools of blue. How sad they were now. I grabbed Becky's hand and hung on for dear life. Inflicting pain no doubt, but she didn't flinch.

"Oh God, Becky," I whispered. "He looks awful! Look at the pain in his eyes!" Tears were rolling down my cheeks.

"I know, Sarah." She turned her head to me. "Remember what he did to you though. It's all right – we'll get through this."

We received our first of what I feared would be many 'Silence in Court!' admonitions. Under any other given circumstances, we'd have giggled about that.

I noticed that Chris too was crying. The judge was having none of it though and told him to pull himself together.

I looked at Mum and Dad, and my sister. They were all sitting bolt upright, glaring at him. I would have done the same in their situation I'm sure. They had nothing but contempt for him and I suddenly felt guilty at my show of emotion. The bastard shot me. He SHOT me.

The prosecution case was one of Attempted Murder. I was stunned when our solicitor had told me that this was what they were going for. Surely not? I did not believe for one minute that Chris had actually tried to kill me. The body of evidence, however, according to my legal team, begged to differ. This was the route to take, they said. I protested feebly but was overruled.

Chris pleaded not guilty of course, which I knew he was going to do, otherwise we wouldn't have been in court at all. The defence's case was that he was not guilty of the allegation due to diminished responsibility. As aghast as I had been at the Attempted Murder accusation, this had shocked me further. He was going to try and get off! He wasn't even man enough to take responsibility and accept his punishment.

Could I blame him for trying though? He knew what he'd done. He'd have to live with it for the rest of his life. Maybe that was punishment enough.

Was being drunk an accepted state for 'diminished responsibility'? Or were there other factors that his barrister was going to bring into play? My head was spinning and part of me wished I'd spent some of my incarceration learning the whys and wherefores of our legal system. All would become clear in due course, I concluded.

Once the opening statements had been outlined, Becky

was called as the prosecution's first witness. She was brilliant, of course. She spoke of the many times he'd abused me and how I'd escaped to her flat on more than one occasion. She told the court about the time he'd pulled me down the stairs and I'd injured my ankle. Mum's head went down at this point, and I could see she was fighting tears. Again, feelings of guilt emerged for putting all of this on my family and friends. Becks went on to say, under questioning, that I had tried many times to get him to seek help for his alcoholism. She concluded by saying that I was a lovely person who couldn't have done more to save my marriage and that what Chris had done to me was abhorrent. She glared at him as she left the stand, but he didn't see. His head was in his hands.

Geoff, our neighbour was called next. I was very interested to hear what he had to say. He averted his eyes from both me and Chris. I felt a bit sorry for him. Until I heard my barrister asking him to confirm that the rifle in our house which Chris apparently owned, was actually licensed to Geoff. Had he not thought to ask Chris about the criminal record that prevented him from owning a gun? Yes, apparently he had. Chris had told him it was an old drink/driving conviction. Does that prevent you from owning a gun? Who knows. Geoff obviously didn't. No mention of the assault conviction by Chris, of course. But I still felt that Geoff was stupid to agree to the plan.

He was asked about Chris's demeanour and behaviour when they were out on their shooting expeditions. He said he was mainly jovial, good fun, the life and soul…etc etc. Upon more detailed questioning, he confirmed that Chris's drinking had got out of hand on a few occasions and that he'd picked an argument with someone in the pub once. They'd all been thrown out as a consequence. When he was cross-examined, the defence barrister tried to make light of this by saying it was all just good-natured high jinks really, wasn't it? Big mistake. Geoff went on to elaborate about Chris's behaviour in the pub, which was clearly way beyond 'high jinks'. It was the type of behaviour that was very familiar to me.

At the end of Geoff's questioning, the judge announced that he would be receiving a fine and would have his own rifle licence revoked. He wanted to put out the message that it was not OK to obtain a rifle in your own name and then hand it over to someone else. Geoff left the stand with his proverbial tail between his legs. Lucy was not present, I noticed.

I was surprised to see some of our workmates called as witnesses. They all spoke of Chris's renowned temper and how unpleasant he could be if things didn't go his way. Each one had his or her own story to tell of a bad run-in with Chris, which was an eye-opener to me, I can tell you. One of them even mentioned the much-invoked office mantra, 'don't get Chris cross'. I had no idea half of these things had gone on. They also told of his drink problem, the fact that he was suspended from work for a while and of his obvious jealousy of my awards' success. Chris glared at a couple of them, momentarily reverting to true form. I glanced at the jury. A few of them had clocked it.

Phil was one of the agency staff who took the stand. I was so pleased to see him that I almost called out. He'd been in touch with me several times since the 'event' but I hadn't actually seen him. Dear Phil, my guardian angel. He left the judge and jury in no doubt as to his thoughts and feelings on the accused – both in terms of his own dealings with the man and in what he had witnessed between Chris and me at the Agency and at various award ceremonies. Chris saved his most acid glare for Phil. He also glanced over at his representative whilst Phil was on the stand, and gave an almost imperceptible nod. His barrister caught it and made a note of something on his pad. I was intrigued.

Phil was the only witness that the defence chose to cross-examine. Chris's barrister attempted to make out that Phil was jealous of Chris and coveted his job. Nice try, Chris! He also suggested that Phil would say anything against Chris because he was in love with me! I laughed out loud! Another 'Silence in Court!' was handed out. After Phil's initial crass attempt at seducing me, he'd never tried it on again. I knew Phil didn't harbour those kind of feelings for me. It was obvious to anyone who worked with him that he was in love with Tina. To his credit, Phil handled the questions very well. He just stated the truth. I guess it's easy to be credible when you're telling the truth. He resisted what I felt must have been a compelling urge to smirk at Chris when he left the stand. Instead he totally ignored him.

The first day's proceedings eventually came to an end, and I was exhausted. I returned home with my family for a hearty meal and what I hoped would be a sleep-inducing cup of cocoa. It wasn't. Perhaps I should have tried a couple of whiskeys instead. I was up the next day. On the stand that is. I felt like crap.

CHAPTER FIFTY-THREE

Mum suggested I take a couple of tranquilisers to steady my nerves, but I wanted to be fully-functioning. As functioning as possible, given the circumstances.

I was called around mid-morning. Shortly after my surgeon had been on the stand to give evidence about my injuries. That was tough to hear, even though I was all too familiar with what my body had gone through. I heard my name being called but wasn't able to move. Becky nudged me and Dad stood up to help me out of my seat. I was still walking with a stick at this stage but decided to dispense with it. I felt that the jury, despite having just heard my surgeon's report, might think I was putting it on. Instead I limped my way to the stand which, in retrospect, was probably worse than using the stick.

I could see that Chris was truly shocked by what he saw. He'd had his head down the whole time the surgeon was detailing my injuries, but now he was looking directly at me. Aside from the limp, I still had my right arm in plaster. The one that I'd broken on his sodding mother's sodding coffee table. And I guess I looked like shit generally. I held Chris's look for a moment but then turned away and focused on getting to the stand without falling on my backside.

We'd rehearsed the questions the barrister was going to ask me, time and time again. Even so, it was like I was hearing them for the first time. I looked at Becky and she nodded encouragingly at me. I stood up a little taller, gammy leg notwithstanding, and lifted my head a little higher. I could do this. The judge had given me permission to sit down but I was determined to stay on my feet for as long as I was able.

Under the careful questioning, I gave a picture of Chris's and my life together. I wanted to show that we'd had some very good times; that we'd been happy for a while. I detailed all the abuse, the jealousy, what happened at our wedding, the AA meetings and the counselling we'd received. I told them about Chris's unfounded jealousy over my working relationship with James. I pointed out that Chris had tried to change his life but that alcohol always eventually won out over me. I knew this would get a vote of sympathy from the jury. It was the truth though.

The defence counsel hurled several 'Objections' at us throughout my questioning, but the judge overruled most of them.

I was to be cross-examined though. Shit. Now I was scared. My barrister had prepared me for this too, but even he didn't know exactly what I was going to be asked.

"Mrs Hobson, is it true that you carried on drinking in front of my client while he was attending AA meetings?"

I was shocked, firstly, at being addressed as Mrs Hobson. Granted we were still married, but…really??

"Well, yes occasionally, but I…"

"Do you think that was a supportive thing to do Mrs Hobson? What kind of an impact do you think that had on your husband?"

This line of questioning hadn't come up in our rehearsals.

"Umm, I did it very rarely actually."

"Very rarely, you say. Isn't even once enough to put pressure on your husband? Your so-called beloved whom you were trying so hard to help?"

The bastard.

"Well I…"

"And did you or did you not, on more than one occasion, go out drinking with your friend Miss Thompson here," he gesticulated towards Becky at this point. "Coming home worse for wear, or returning the next day with a hangover?"

A hugely indignant Becky leapt to her feet. "Objection!"

A ripple of laughter echoed around the room.

The judge lowered his glasses and looked directly at Becky. "You are not allowed to raise objections, Miss Thompson. That is for the professionals. Please sit down."

I grinned at Becky. "Once or twice maybe, yes," I answered.

"And how do you think that affected your husband, Mrs Hobson? The husband you say you were trying to keep off the booze?"

"Objection! Unnecessary and unfair line of questioning!" This time from the professional.

"Overruled!"

I glared at the judge. He seemed to be enjoying this!

"And is it true to say that you flaunted your success, your award wins, in your husband's face?"

"Absolutely not!" I was furious. "Quite the opposite actually. I was sorry that-"

"You revelled in your wins, didn't you? Knowing that it was bound to affect your husband's self-confidence."

"Objection!" Counsel cannot claim to know the witness's mind!"

"Sustained."

Thank God. Finally!

"And furthermore, Mrs Hobson, you didn't try to hide your relationship with young Mr..." He consulted his notes. "Mr Cunningham, did you? You flaunted that in your husband's face too."

"But I..."

"How do you think that made him feel?"

"My relationship with James was..."

"An extra-marital one, yes. Yet another thing for your poor husband to have to deal with. No wonder he was driven to the state he ended up in on Friday, 23rd March. No further questions, Your Honour."

We had rehearsed questions about James. The one thing my barrister had tried to drum into me was never to start a sentence with the words 'My relationship with James...' Shit. I'd fallen at a basic hurdle.

I looked over apologetically at my long-suffering representative, but he just smiled sweetly. Had I blown it?

The second day was over though, thank God. Becky gave me a reassuring hug and told me I was doing great. Yeah, great apart from the glaring fucking blunder. She said not to worry about that, the jury will determine the truth. She reckoned Chris's 'bastard of a solicitor' was simply trying to make a case where there clearly wasn't one. I wished I had her confidence.

CHAPTER FIFTY-FOUR

At home, after another warming meal and this time a fair bit of accompanying alcohol, we all collapsed in front of the telly to watch a Morecombe and Wise rerun. We had agreed on something light-hearted and entertaining, something to take our minds off the day's proceedings. My family all echoed Becky's platitudes of how well I was doing and how well it was going generally. For my part I wished I could take the stand again tomorrow and make a better job of it.

One by one we all fell asleep during the programme. I don't think it was a comment on the standard of the show, more a result of total exhaustion from our emotions having been run ragged. Possibly helped by a large consumption of wine. Dad soon started snoring like a trooper, which woke the rest of us up. Surmising that any further TV viewing was not really an option, we instead opted for an early night and were all tucked up by 10:00 p.m. I immediately fell into a deep sleep, but awoke with a start at around 2:30 and remained wide awake for a good hour. I couldn't stop my head spinning with everything. Would I ever know a sweet night's sleep again?

The next day dawned early but none too bright. I hoped

this wasn't a bad omen. The prosecution's case was over, it was now down to the defence to prove Chris's plea of diminished responsibility. I wondered briefly what other nasty tricks his barrister had up his sleeve.

A few of Chris's friends were called first, including Dodgy Dan, whom Jane had spent our wedding night with. Did Chris know about this brief liaison, I wondered? Not relevant of course. Not in the slightest.

They were all, unsurprisingly, very supportive of Chris. Said he was a great guy and that what he'd done was totally out of character. They acknowledged that he liked a drink but not one of them referred to it as a 'problem'. I looked over at my barrister. Surely he was going to cross-examine?

Indeed he was. Dan was the chosen one. He was asked to recount the events of our wedding evening, from around 11:00 p.m. onwards. Funnily enough, Chris's lawyer hadn't brought this up. Dan tried his best, but under clever questioning he had to admit that yes, Chris had not been very nice to me. Yes, he had shouted at me. Yes, he had told me to 'fuck off to bed by myself'. This elicited a gasp from some of the jury members and an extremely indignant look from my Dad. I could see he was furious. Dodgy Dan then made the mistake of saying that I had deserved it because I'd ignored Chris for most of the evening, preferring to dance the night away with my friends. My lawyer left an impactful silence for a good few seconds.

"Are you really saying, Mr O'Connor, that Ms Williams (I had asked him to please use my maiden name in court) deserved to be told to 'fuck off' on her wedding night by her new husband simply because she'd spent part of the evening on the dance floor? Are you saying that Mr O'Connor?"

"Well, I thought it was…"

"Because if you are, God help the poor girl who says 'I do' to you."

A slight titter arose from the courtroom. Becky emitted a sotto voce 'Yes!' and we looked at each other and grinned. Nice one! A bit below the belt maybe, but certainly deserved, I felt.

"I put it to you, Mr O'Connor, that Mr Hobson's behaviour on that night towards his wife was not becoming of a newly married man. It was the type of behaviour that we've heard in court he exhibited towards his wife many times, through no fault of her own. The cause was always the same. Excessive drinking and Mr Hobson's nasty change of character which often accompanied said excessive drinking. No further questions."

I began to feel a bit more comfortable about the way things were going. Chris only really had his friends to vouch for him. I wondered if his Mum was going to take the stand, but it didn't look like it. They must have weighed that one up carefully. On the one hand she would be a great witness for Chris's character and could no doubt have milked his 'sad' upbringing without the presence of a Dad. On the other hand though, how much credence would you give a mother's testimony about her son? Most mothers would willingly die for their sons. Also, having seen the way she'd crumbled under Becky's telling off, I suspected that the defence team was not confident in her ability to survive cross-questioning. Shame. I had a few questions I'd have liked to have put to her myself.

My newfound confidence was short-lived however, because the next witness called to the stand by the defence was a psychiatrist. I was not expecting that. He clearly had no axe to grind, no side to take. Was he going to throw the cat amongst the pigeons?

Well this fancy professional with his smart suit, oversized tie and several initials after his name was indeed the business. He had apparently examined Chris after he was arrested and gave a convincing report as to his state of mind. When asked directly by Chris's barrister whether he thought Chris was of diminished responsibility when he shot me, he replied that in his professional opinion he was. Shit. Can one argue with a professional opinion? I guess another professional could. Trouble was, we didn't have a professional on our team. Not a psychiatric one at least. Bit of an oversight I feared. My barrister, perhaps unwisely, decided to cross-examine.

"How can you be sure, Dr Stevens, that Mr Hobson exhibited diminished responsibility? Is that not just an excuse for his behaviour?"

Silence. Accompanied by a deathly stare from Dr Stevens.

"I don't offer nor do I sanction *excuses*. I am a professional and I give my professional opinion, which is based on 23 years of study and practice."

Fair enough I suppose.

"I appreciate that of course Dr Stevens, but is it possible you could be wrong?"

Oh good Lord.

"My dear man, I am not wrong. I have outlined the symptoms Mr Hobson was displaying when I examined him, which were quite in keeping with a person acting out of diminished responsibility. Do you want me to go through them again?"

My lawyer pressed on regardless, seemingly oblivious to the cavernous hole he was digging himself.

"Your findings though, Dr Stevens, were they all based on medical facts or was there an element of your personal opinion thrown in there too?"

"A psychiatrist's opinion is generally based on facts. Facts that he has learned, facts that he has observed. You can't really separate the two. Just because I'm saying what you don't want to hear doesn't make it incorrect, nor does it make it an opinion rather than fact. I have given my report and my evidence."

Our man shuffled his notes. I wished he'd just sit down and shut up.

"But I must ask you again about opinion versus medical facts. Could it be-"

"Objection! My colleague is badgering the expert witness and doubting his credentials!"

"Sustained."

Thank God.

"No further questions, my Lord."

Well that was great, wasn't it? I think he possibly did more harm than good with that little interlude. I snuck a look over at the jury. They didn't look too impressed either.

"Fuck's sake!" Becky whispered. "What the hell is he playing at?"

I could offer no response. Nor did I have time to think about it further because I heard a familiar name being called to the stand. Mr Christopher Hobson. This was it. I'd have to hear his voice. Worse, I'd have to hear him trying to worm his way out of taking any responsibility for his actions.

It started off tame enough. His lawyer asked him various

240

questions about his early life, our time together, his work etc. Chris answered in a quiet but confident manner. He glanced over at the jury from time to time and I witnessed a couple of the female members falling under the spell of his pools of blue. Bugger. Granted he didn't milk it, but he knew the effect he was having on them.

He skated over the father's absence in his life and actually gave scant detail about his childhood. I felt certain our barrister – even though it had to be said that I'd lost a little confidence in him – would question him about his upbringing. It was surely relevant.

It was pretty tough listening to his voice but I found it impossible to look at him. I focused my attention on my lap instead, trying to quell the tremor in my legs. Becky grabbed my arm – my non-plastered one – and hung on tight.

It was progressing fairly predictably. I learned nothing new. The jury, although attentive, learned nothing new either. The next question, however, refocused their minds as they, to a man, leaned forward in anticipation of Chris's response.

"Could you take the court through the events of Friday 27th March please, Mr Hobson."

His voice became quieter as he recounted coming home from work early that day. He'd had a row with someone at the office and decided to have a drink before I arrived home, just to calm his nerves. One drink turned into two, then three and more while he waited for me. Now angry that I was so late, he convinced himself that I was with 'that young boy'. He couldn't say his name until prompted by his lawyer to be more specific. When asked what had made him take the rifle out of its cabinet he just shrugged and said he didn't know. He didn't recall doing it.

Oh really Chris?

Although I still couldn't look him in the eye, I had raised my head a little, intent on catching every word. His voice was barely audible as he recited details of my return from work, the ensuing argument and, finally, the shooting.

I shut my eyes. God, it was hard to listen to. Becky squeezed my arm tightly and Dad put his hand on my shoulder. I wasn't sure I could stick much more of this.

But then it happened.

"What drove you to these actions Mr Hobson? Would you say you were under tremendous emotional stress, caused by your wife?"

"Bastard!" Becky hissed.

The ensuing silence was so long that his barrister repeated the question. You could have heard a pin drop in court.

"No."

His representative's head snapped up from his notes.

"I'll repeat the question Mr Hobson. Would you say you were under tremendous…"

"No." A little louder this time. "The only pressure I was under was brought on by me. By my own actions. This was not Sarah's fault."

A collective gasp from the jury. A distinct look of thunder from his barrister.

"Your Honour, could I take a moment with my client please?"

"I don't need a moment, I have to say this. Sarah – please look at me."

I slowly raised my head.

"I am so sorry, Sarah. I never meant to hurt you. It was the drink, work, my ridiculous jealousy. My inability to fully enjoy life without alcohol. But it wasn't your fault. None of it. It was all my doing and I deserve whatever's coming to me."

I looked into his beautiful blue eyes, now brimming with tears, and saw the man I'd fallen in love with. I saw his weaknesses yes, but I also saw his worth, his humour, his kindness. We stared at each other, oblivious to his barrister's unceasing protestations.

"Sarah, I love you. I am so sorry for what I did to you. You will never know how sorry I am."

His representative sat down, defeated. After a few moments of silence, Chris was instructed to leave the witness box.

I whispered something to my barrister who jumped to his feet and asked the judge if I could take the stand again. It was greeted with a feeble 'Objection!' from the defence which was thankfully overruled.

I limped to the box and was reminded by the judge that I was still under oath. Whatever, mate.

All eyes were on me.

I looked directly at Chris, smiled at him and gave a little nod. I then turned my attention to the judge. I've no idea where I got the strength or courage from.

"Your Honour, I believe this man needs help, not punishment. Our marriage is over, we are finished, but I don't want him to go to prison for what he did to me. Please get him some help."

I managed to keep it together until I was safely back in my seat. Once there I promptly burst into tears and sobbed like a baby.

The summing up formalities followed, together with the judge's instructions to the jury. They were then told to retire to consider their verdict. Court was to be reconvened in the morning.

I could tell that my family and Becky were somewhat stunned by my intervention but they withheld any criticism. They were unanimously elated that Chris had finally taken responsibility for his actions.

"Fair play," commented Becky. "Didn't think the bastard had it in him."

Dad was less circumspect. "'Bout time the nasty coward owned his evil crime."

That night we talked about anything and everything except the case. I wasn't able to contribute much to the general chit-chat. I was exhausted and fell into bed soon after supper, afraid of what the next day might bring.

Chapter Fifty-five

With the court assembled, the judge wasted no time in summoning the jury. He asked them if they'd reached a verdict. The head juror confirmed that they had. Was it unanimous? It was.

"On the charge of Attempted Murder, how do you find the defendant?"

"Guilty Your Honour."

A long, pitiful wail, which sounded like an animal in distress, broke the ensuing silence. For a second I thought it had emanated from me. But no, it was Chris's Mum. Of course. She was in bits. Someone helped her from the court and I admit I actually felt a little sorry for the woman.

As for me, I couldn't quite compute my reaction to the verdict. Pleased? Not pleased? Which was it? Hadn't a clue. Becky and my family were all smiling and hugging me. Our barrister was shaking hands with everyone and congratulating his team. He looked a little smug to me. Or was it relieved? Considering he'd nearly cocked it up big time with the psychiatrist.

I looked over at Chris. He hadn't moved. His head was still down and his shoulders slumped. He must have felt me staring at him. He slowly raised his head and looked at me with his beautiful blue eyes. We held each other's gaze, like a moment frozen in time whilst madness and chaos reigned about us. Then he gave me a little smile and a nod. My heart broke. It was like he was saying it's OK, I know what I did and I deserve this.

The judge called us all to order. He was about to hand out the sentence. We hadn't anticipated this; our barrister said that sentencing would most likely take place at a later date. Clearly our judge was a busy man and wanted to get this done and dusted.

We all took our seats again, apart from Chris who was instructed to remain standing. I was terrified. I didn't quite know what to expect to hear from the judge. My team hadn't discussed what kind of sentencing might be handed down on a guilty verdict. I was suddenly consumed with the thought of Chris spending years and years in prison. I gripped Becky's hand again.

I think it's fair to say that what ensued surprised everyone in the courtroom. Not least the accused. The judge said that he had taken into account Chris's declaration and he had also noted my plea. He felt that, a previous conviction notwithstanding, the accused was generally a good person who changed character when he drank too much. Bearing that in mind, and considering the amount of time he'd already spent in jail prior to the trial, he was deferring sentencing for a year with the following stipulation; Chris must agree to a six month spell in a rehabilitation centre. He was to undergo a psyche report from two psychiatrists before his release and he was not to come within 500 yards of me or contact me ever again. In the following six months, he must demonstrate that he was a changed man. He set another court date for one year hence, and then asked Chris's barrister if he was in agreement with this. After a brief consultation with his client, the barrister confirmed that he was.

I didn't really understand what the hell was going on, but I grasped that Chris wasn't going to jail for the time being anyway. I started crying. Becky hugged me. "It's OK Sarah, it's all over now. You never have to face him again."

I cried even more. Becky always had my back but she never fully appreciated the fact that I loved Chris dearly. I knew I would never see him again, but that just made me desperately sad. I didn't want any of this.

I didn't want to be the person who'd been shot by her husband. I didn't want to be the victim here. I just wanted my Chris back. The Chris that I'd fallen in love with.

"Sarah!" Chris was being led out of the court. "Sarah!"

I looked up.

"I'm sorry, darling. I love you."

I looked into his sad, sad pools of blue for the last time. "I love you too, Chris."

ACKNOWLEDGEMENTS

A huge thank you to my son Patrick for editing the book and for, I'm sure, resisting the temptation to rewrite most of it. Thank you also to my other talented son, Alex, for the beautiful cover illustration, and to Irene Paradisi for her expertise in completing the front cover design. Thank you to Sian Langley for helping with the legal stuff. Last but not least a big thank you to all my friends, with a special mention for Claire Bunbury, who encouraged, badgered and shamed me into finally finishing my debut novel. I'm forever indebted to you. You'll be delighted to know that a second one is in the pipeline!

About the Author

Sue Ryan spent several years working in the London Advertising business in the '80s. She met her husband, Nick, at Lintas London Advertising Agency. A jingle writer and radio producer, Nick wrote and produced the very first Just One Cornetto jingle. They have two sons; Patrick is a Writer/Director and Alex a professional Musician. In the year 2000, Sue and Nick took the strange decision to move their family from Leigh-on-Sea in Essex to County Kerry in Southern Ireland. Sue remains there to this day with her cat Sasha, halfway up a mountain surrounded by sheep and cows. Sadly Nick passed away in May 2022.